**"Thank goodness you're here, Doc,"
his receptionist said.
"I was beginning to think
you weren't coming.**

"We didn't have a clue what to do with all the calls for appointments."

"Appointments?" Eric walked in to find the tiny office filled with pets and their owners, the great majority of whom were women.

"All right," he said to the tech when she shut the door behind them. "What's going on?"

"My guess is they're all here to see you."

"Me?" Eric shook his head.

"You haven't read the paper yet?"

"Why does everyone care whether I've read the paper yet?" he thundered.

The tech gestured to the folded copy of the *Gazette* on the corner of his desk. "See for yourself." She paused. "You might want to sit down."

He did and then carefully opened the paper to read the headline. "Daddy's Little Matchmakers."

## KATHLEEN Y'BARBO

RITA® and Carol Award nominee Kathleen Y'Barbo is the bestselling author of more than forty novels, novellas and young adult books. In all, more than one million copies of her books are currently in print in the U.S. and abroad.

Kathleen is a member of Romance Writers of America and American Christian Fiction Writers.

A tenth-generation Texan, Kathleen Y'Barbo has a daughter and three grown sons. She recently added her own hero in combat boots—who came with five sons and two daughters of his own—and is proud to be an Air Force wife even if it did mean giving up her Texas driver's license.

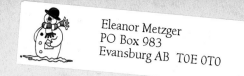
# Daddy's Little Matchmakers

## Kathleen Y'Barbo

Recycling programs
for this product may
not exist in your area.

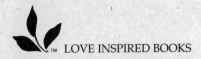 LOVE INSPIRED BOOKS

ISBN-13: 978-0-373-08219-3

DADDY'S LITTLE MATCHMAKERS

www.LoveInspiredBooks.com

**Printed in U.S.A.**

Dear Reader,

Welcome to Love Inspired!

2012 is a very special year for us. It marks the fifteenth anniversary of Love Inspired. Hard to believe that fifteen years ago, we first began publishing our warm and wonderful inspirational romances.

Back in 1997, we offered readers three books a month. Since then we've expanded quite a bit! In addition to the heartwarming contemporary romances of Love Inspired, we have the exciting romantic suspenses of Love Inspired Suspense, and the adventurous historical romances of Love Inspired Historical. Whatever your reading preference, we've got fourteen books a month for you to choose from now!

Throughout the year we'll be celebrating in several different ways. Look for books by bestselling authors who've been writing for us since the beginning, stories by brand-new authors you won't want to miss, special miniseries in all three lines, reissues of top authors and much, much more.

This is our way of thanking you for reading Love Inspired books. We know our uplifting stories of hope, faith and love touch your hearts as much as they touch ours.

Join us in celebrating fifteen amazing years of inspirational romance!

Blessings,

Melissa Endlich and Tina James
Senior Editors of Love Inspired Books

To my "other daughters":
The fabulous Lindley LeBlanc, RN,
whose sentence was endlessly brilliant!
And the amazing Erica Puckett, love you darlin!
Gig'em, girls!

\* \* \*

Fathers, do not exasperate your children;
instead, bring them up in the training
and instruction of the Lord.
—*Ephesians* 6:4

# *Chapter One*

The call came in a full fifteen minutes before Amy Spencer's lunch break ended. As a temp, she had no obligation to go beyond the requirements of the job she would have only until Friday. And yet, how could she ignore the phone when it was the first time the thing had rung all morning?

Reluctantly she set aside the remains of her sandwich and the novel she'd likely finish before the end of the day. "*Vine Beach Gazette,* Classifieds Department," she said as she reached for her water bottle and took a sip.

"I would like to place an ad to sell my sailboat."

Much as the distinctly male voice stated his

desire firmly, there seemed to be the slightest bit of hesitancy there. This gave Amy pause to check the caller ID.

Eric Wilson. The new veterinarian who'd bought the clinic across the street from the *Gazette*. Handsome, single and the father of three little girls who sat beside him in church every Sunday.

"So," he continued, "how would I go about placing an ad?"

Scrolling to the correct place on her computer screen, Amy read him the particulars. "You can either go online and do it yourself or I can take down the details and place it for you. Or you could come in and place the ad and pay for it then." She waited a moment. Nothing but silence and the occasional bark of a dog on the other end of the phone. "Dr. Wilson?" she finally asked.

"Yes, I'm sorry," he said quickly. "I was just trying to decide."

"Whether to sell, or whether to place the ad yourself?"

"Actually, I—" An eruption of high-pitched squeals interrupted his statement. "Girls, please. I'm on the phone," he said before returning to her. "Thank you for the information. You've been a great help but I'm afraid I'm going to have to—"

And then the line went dead.

Amy hung up the phone thinking of what sort of chaos three daughters might bring into the life of one single man. Having grown up the only child of older parents, she had nothing to compare.

Rising to step away from her desk, Amy tossed her sandwich into the trash and grabbed her book. With the sun shining, the sea breeze blowing and the heat of summer not yet unbearable, she decided to spend the remaining ten minutes of her lunch break reading in the shade on her favorite park bench.

Beneath the canopy of green leaves, she scooted to the far end of the bench and settled into a comfortable position. From her vantage point, she could see the blue-green waters of the Gulf of Mexico and the whitecaps rolling up on Vine Beach a quarter of a mile to the south. She could also witness comings and goings in both directions on Vine Beach's primary north–south thoroughfare, aptly named Main Street.

With little to recommend Vine Beach beyond the smattering of beachfront rentals and the tiny harbor, the main traffic on the street consisted of locals. No one seemed to mind, though members of the local Chamber of Commerce met on occasion to debate ways to bring in more traffic. As yet, nothing had come of these meetings so the city remained a sleepy coastal town.

Across the way, Amy spied the elderly beautician unlocking the garishly pink doors of Ima's Beauty Shop and waved. Ima returned the gesture before slipping inside. Next door a painter was putting the final touches on the new sign on the Wilson Animal Clinic's front window. She thought of Eric Wilson's call and wondered which of the several dozen boats at the harbor was his.

Another check of her watch and Amy set aside her novel to lean back against the bench to look up through the canopy of oak leaves at the brilliant blue sky above. Returning to Vine Beach as an adult had been much different than she'd expected. Every summer for as long as she could remember, Amy had spent as much time as she could with her grandparents in their cottage by the beach.

Roses flourished on the arbor and the garden always provided enough to make porch salad, but her favorite memories were of sitting with her grandmother on the swing beneath the arbor. Her sandy toes barely brushing the ground, she could while away the hours watching the waves and the occasional sailboat heading for shore. At night she slept with the window open to the ocean breeze and dreamed salt-tinged dreams about happily-ever-afters beneath the upstairs rafters.

Never had she expected to live there, albeit temporarily, as an adult. But when her grandmother's hip surgery required she have a caregiver, Amy stepped up to the challenge. After all, Mom and Dad had only kept her employed at their shop in Houston out of love. All three of them knew there wasn't near enough work for three florists.

And thus when the call came regarding the surgery, Amy gladly spent the spring caring for her grandmother, tending the garden, the roses and her precious nana in equal parts until all were blooming. Nana's choice to move into Sandy Shores, the new assisted-living community out on Harbor Drive, had surprised Amy. Until, that is, she visited and saw her grandmother had landed solidly in her element. Always the social butterfly, Nana loved being in the middle of everything, something she couldn't manage at home.

Amy took a deep breath and let it out slowly. Nana no longer needed her and, as of tomorrow, neither did the *Gazette*. Was it time to move on? And if so, where would she go?

Across Main Street, the painter completed his work on the clinic door then stepped back to admire the finished product. "Eric Wilson, DVM," she whispered as she read the words beneath the sign.

Amy's thoughts again shifted to Dr. Wilson. Everything she knew about the man came from her grandmother, Nana Spencer, whose knowledge of all things related to Vine Beach was arguably more extensive than any data uncovered by the reporters at the *Gazette*. And according to Nana, the veterinarian, a widower of undetermined length, had moved to Vine Beach to take over Doc Simmons's practice upon the older man's retirement and to see that his girls were near his late wife's family.

A car door slammed, drawing her attention to the parking lot beside the animal clinic. There she saw the object of her thoughts walking toward what was likely the back door of the clinic. He looked busy—possibly distracted by whatever boisterous behavior had caused him to end their call so quickly—as he ran his hand through thick dark hair. He lifted his head, and their gazes met awkwardly across the distance. At least she thought he saw her. For a second Amy wondered if she should acknowledge him. The vet waved, solving the problem of how to respond, so she did the same.

Checking her watch, Amy gathered up her novel and rose. Four more hours of work, and her temporary job at the paper would end. Then she'd be forced to decide whether to allow the temp agency to place her elsewhere or perhaps to pack her things and move on.

Surely there was work for a trained florist somewhere. *Trained florist*. More like a girl who'd picked so many flowers as a child that her mother finally taught her how to make something pretty of her mess. Amy giggled at the thought.

"You have a nice laugh."

She jumped, dropping the novel as she whirled around to see Eric Wilson crossing Main Street. Scrambling for the book, she tugged at the edge of her blouse and tried not to allow her embarrassment to show.

"I'm sorry. I didn't mean to startle you."

His worried expression made her smile in spite of her flustered state. "No, it's fine. Really." She lifted her hand to smooth back her hair and promptly dropped the book again.

The vet leaned to reach for the novel and so did Amy. Before either could accomplish the task, their heads bumped. Wincing, Amy felt the heat rise in her neck. As she took a step backward, Eric retrieved the book.

"I'm sorry," he said again as he thrust the book toward her. "Seems I've now got two reasons to apologize."

"No, really." Amy took the book and held it tight against her chest. "I'm fine." She glanced down at the smudge of brown decorating her blouse and saw the source: a nasty smear of dirt in a matching color on the novel's back cover. She quickly flipped the book around and adjusted its location to cover the spot then slowly lifted her eyes to meet his stare.

An awkward moment passed and then he reached to offer her his hand. "Eric Wilson," he said. "I'm new to Vine Beach." He gestured to the clinic behind him. "Bought the practice from Doc Simmons a few months ago." A pause. "And you're Amy. The classifieds girl."

Amy shook his hand as she pondered the statement. The vet must have noticed her expression of confusion for he hastened to add, "I called back and someone told me Amy the classifieds girl was at lunch. Sitting in the park. Reading a book. And so, since I was on the cell and could plainly see that there was a woman sitting in the park next to the newspaper office reading a book, I…" He released her hand and took a step backward then looked away. "Anyway," he finally said, "I wanted to apologize for hanging up the call so abruptly. Things just got a little noisy and then the dog got loose and, well, I really hadn't intended for them to overhear, anyway."

"Happens all the time," Amy hastened to say as she tried not to study his handsome features or notice the slight hint of what might be tiredness in his eyes. His lovely eyes, she amended.

"Especially lately," he said softly. "What I mean is, the girls are getting settled into their new home and new school, which means things have been a little…"

"Noisy?" she supplied.

"Yes," Dr. Wilson said on a long exhale of breath. "They're good girls, and I'm very glad I've got my mother here to help. But managing three girls while trying to get a vet practice off the ground has been an adventure."

"Your daughters are adorable." At his look of surprise, she shrugged. "I've seen you… that is, them, at church and, well, they're adorable."

"Oh, yes, right." He ran his hand through his hair. "Thankfully they all look like their mother. They miss her, I'm afraid."

Dr. Wilson's eyes widened, and Amy knew he'd given her more insight than he'd intended. She hurried to cover the awkward moment with the first thing she could think of. "It's hard to move with children, I would imagine."

"Yes," he said, seeming grateful for the gentle veer away from what was probably a sore subject. "Though the unpacking was much easier than the packing. It's amazing the amount of things girls collect. Ribbons, bows, dolls and don't get me started on the amount of clothes they have. And the shoes? Why does anyone need more than a dozen pairs of shoes?"

His chuckle was low and swift, and Amy quickly joined in. "Hey, now. We women need our accessories, and a girl can't have her shoes be mismatched with her outfit. It just isn't done."

"Oh, believe me, I know. I suppose they in-herited the shoe gene from their mother. She was forever explaining why she needed yet another pair."

The town clock struck the half hour, and Amy jerked her attention in that direction. Time to return to her desk. "It's my turn to apologize, Dr. Wilson. You see, my lunch hour's over and…" She tilted her head toward the newspaper office. "I should get back to work."

He followed her gaze then, as an expression of recognition dawned, and nodded. "Please, call me Eric."

"Eric," she echoed. "If you'll call me Amy." Shifting her book to the other hand, Amy reached out to shake his. His grip was firm, his smile slow in appearing. "It's been nice meeting you."

The vet seemed unsure of what to say. "Nice, yes," he echoed. "And I'll call again soon, Amy." His eyes widened as he must have realized his word choice left his intentions in question. "To sell the boat," he added. "Probably Monday. I should have a decent photo to use by then."

"Monday. Right." She almost told him that on Monday someone else would be taking his call. Before she could manage it, the vet had turned to sprint back across Main Street. As she watched him go, Amy wondered what it must be like to live in a noisy house. To have to end a call because children were laughing.

Amy sighed. Somewhere out there the Lord

had a place for her. And perhaps there would be a family, as well. Whatever, wherever, she knew she would find that perfect fit. Until then, nothing in her life could be anything less than temporary.

Once again, Eric Wilson turned to wave, and this time she returned the gesture without hesitation. Silently she added a prayer that he, too, would find whatever it was he needed.

Eric Wilson slipped in the back door of the clinic and reached for the lone file awaiting his attention in his in-box then went into his office and closed the door. Unlike his in-box, his mailbox was stuffed full of envelopes, all bills needing to be paid. Eric sighed and settled behind the desk he'd inherited with the building.

Since arriving in Vine Beach and acquiring Dr. Simmons's dwindling practice, he'd found it painfully obvious why the old vet had chosen to retire. There simply weren't enough clients to keep a full-time veterinarian in business.

Of course, he'd known the size of the practice and had ample time to change his mind once he saw the sorry state of the ledger sheet, but coming to Vine Beach meant giving up some things. Financial solvency and his prize sailboat would just have to be sacrificed in the short term so his girls would be settled and happy in the long term.

It was a fair trade, though he would miss that sailboat dearly.

Perhaps he should call now and get it over with. He could always upload a photo of the craft tonight from his laptop. Surely he had a decent one saved somewhere. Besides, it would not be any easier to put the boat up for sale on Monday. Likely he would find too many good reasons to keep it instead.

Eric reached for the phone then decided the classifieds girl was probably not back at her desk. Amy, that was her name. And she was pretty. Eyes as blue as the sky and blond hair that fell in heavy curls over her shoulders. This much he'd allowed himself to notice. Anything more just felt wrong. As if he was somehow being unfaithful to his wife's memory.

And yet his friends all told him to get on with his life. Just this morning his mother had gently reminded him it had been more than three years since Christy's long battle with cancer had been lost. And then there were the seemingly nonstop questions from the girls regarding his single state and when they might expect him to fall in love again.

The trouble with all the good advice was that none of it felt as if it applied to him. As for the girls and their questions, what did they know of love? It wasn't as if he could just shut off his feelings at will. In truth, Eric wasn't completely sure how he felt about any of it.

Worse, the more days that passed the fewer memories he could recollect about life before cancer changed everything. Not everything, he corrected. The girls were still the same. Slightly more subdued when he tried to talk to them about Christy, but all in all just as lovely and lively as they had been before.

Their resiliency humbled him, as did their repeated promises to him that God would bring him another wife. Not a girlfriend, they always insisted, for he told them he would never date, but a wife. A wife to make him happy again.

A tear threatened and he blinked it away.

That his girls were concerned with his happiness spoke volumes, though he couldn't yet agree with their idea of a solution. Perhaps his mother and the others were right. Maybe he just needed to get over it and move on.

But how? It sounded so easy in theory, but in reality, Eric knew he was well and truly stuck. Hadn't his old friend Riley said the same thing just yesterday on the phone? Pride hadn't allowed Eric to answer, or maybe it was the fact that once again Riley was trying to convince him to join the widowers' small group that met on Saturday mornings.

He didn't need a small group to remind him he was a widower. And he surely didn't need to hang around a basketball court with a bunch of other guys talking about death and dying.

Eric ran his hand through his hair and leaned back to close his eyes. A moment later, he opened them again, his gaze landing on the stack of bills. Yet another problem he had not solved.

What he could do, however, was see to the lone client who was waiting for him in exam room one. With a sigh, he forced his mind to focus on the details of the file on his desk then went to see to the ailing terrier. At least a broken bone was something he could fix, unlike the troubles that seemed to pile on like stones on a very tall and completely impass- able wall.

# Chapter Two

Amy returned to her desk with the veterinarian on her mind. Absently, she swiped at the faint brown stain on her blouse, now slightly damp after a scrubbing in the ladies' room sink, as she looked out the window across Main Street to the clinic. Settling into her chair, she spied the message light blinking and reached for the phone.

"How much is an ad?" the cutest little voice asked. A pause and then came whispering that Amy couldn't quite decipher. "There's no one there, Grammy." Finally the girl gave a phone number. Twice.

Smiling, Amy wrote down the number then

placed the return call. An older woman answered with a firm, "Hello?"

"Yes," Amy said, "I received a call about placing an ad." She paused. "But I believe it was from a child so…"

"Oh, yes," the woman said. "Of course. Just a moment and I'll put Hailey on."

"All right," Amy said as she wondered what was going on.

"Hello" came the voice from the answering machine message. "I, that is, *we* would like to place an ad. How much will that cost?"

"It depends." Amy clicked over to the proper screen on her computer. "What sort of ad would you like to place?"

A moment of silence followed, and then the shared whispers of several other voices came across the line. Apparently this would be a group effort.

"Hello?" Amy said. "Is anyone there?"

"Yes, ma'am" came the shaky response.

"All right, then." Amy placed her fingers on the keyboard. "First I need your full name and address so I can set up the account." When the girl complied, Amy said, "All right, then,

Hailey Wilson, go ahead and tell me what you'd like the ad to say."

"We would like to place an ad for our daddy, Dr. Wilson." Someone with a similar girlish voice shouted a correction. "No, I mean for someone," the child amended.

Another voice, also quite young, added, "For someone for our daddy."

*Dr. Wilson.* Amy grinned. *Eric Wilson's girls were setting him up? Interesting.* She checked the caller ID. The number came up as belonging to Susan Wilson, likely the woman who answered the phone.

A squeal from the other end of the line drew Amy's attention back to the situation at hand. "Before I can process your request, you'll need to put your daddy on," Amy said.

"Well, I can't exactly do that." A pause, this time without any background noise beyond a barking dog. "My daddy is unable to come to the phone. He just went back to work. But he's the best daddy in the world," she added. "He braids our hair and bakes cookies with us. He's gonna teach me to sail someday when I'm bigger."

Something in the sincerity in their voices

softened Amy's heart. While there wasn't a chance she could possibly place such an ad, she'd begun to think the idea of it was the sweetest thing she'd heard all day. "I see. He sounds like a wonderful daddy. Now why don't you put your babysitter on the phone and she can have your wonderful daddy call back when he gets home?"

"We don't have a babysitter. Just our Grammy."

Amy let out a long breath. This must be Susan. "Then might I speak to your grammy?"

"No, don't do that!" was quickly followed by a crash that sounded like breaking glass. Then came a dog's excited yip.

A scream, and then the line went dead.

Amy held on to the receiver for a moment then slowly returned it to its cradle. What had just happened?

She reached to return her computer screen to the home page and tried to shrug off the sense that something just wasn't right. What if the elderly woman who answered the phone was in distress? Amy thought of her grandmother's fall and how blessed she was to have neighbors who checked on her.

What if Susan Wilson had fallen and now lay helpless with only Eric's little girls to assist? Would they know what to do? The thought sent her into action. Quickly she hit redial and listened as the phone rang repeatedly then went to an automated voice mail.

Amy jotted down the address the girl had given her and snagged her purse. If anyone in Vine Beach needed to place a classified, they'd just have to wait. Besides, what could the managing editor do, fire her? She had only a few more hours of work left, anyway.

"I'll be right back," Amy said as she passed Bev Calloway's open door.

The city reporter looked up from her computer, her glasses dangling precariously on the end of her nose. "Emergency?"

"I hope not." Amy hitched her purse up higher on her shoulder. "I got a call I'd like to check out. Older lady and some kids. Heard a crash that sounded like glass breaking and now I can't get anyone to answer."

She thought about mentioning the identity of the woman, maybe telling Bev to call the vet clinic, then decided against it. If she was wrong, she'd look like a fool. Better to check things out first and apologize later if need be.

Bev's dark brows rose. "Should I call an ambulance?"

"I don't think so. Not yet, anyway. The address is just around the corner." Her fingers found the keys. "Might want to say a little prayer, though. I'm hoping it's nothing, but you never know."

"Will do," Bev called as Amy hurried out the building to her car.

A few minutes later, she made the turn and soon found herself in front of a tidy redbrick home trimmed in white and marked by a front door of glossy dark green. An empty driveway ended at a matching garage with a basketball goal hung just over the center of the double-size door.

Pulling to the curb across the street, Amy shifted the car into Park. The black mailbox at the curb had the name Wilson emblazoned in slightly mismatched alphabet stickers, the only sign of imperfection in what was an otherwise perfect abode.

Amy spied a black-and-white Springer

Spaniel bounding down the driveway toward her followed in quick succession by a stair-stepped trio of fair-haired girls—the same ones she remembered from church. Eric Wilson's daughters.

The tallest of the three carried a leash as if she might use it to lasso the spaniel while the other two, lagging behind their sister by a few paces, seemed to have assumed a supporting role in the drama. All were headed toward the street.

"Stop right there!" Amy called as she turned off the engine and fumbled for the door handle. "Do *not* follow that dog into the street!"

Throwing open the door, Amy jumped out and looked both ways across the empty street. Then she hurried to head off the oncoming parade of fair-haired children by snagging the dog's collar and guiding him back onto the lawn.

"Hand me the leash, please," she said to the eldest of the trio.

The child complied while her sisters waited at the edge of the driveway. Only after she had the animal safely corralled did Amy consider that the pup might not have taken kindly to her intervention.

After giving the dog a pat on the head, Amy glanced over at the girls who stood very still on the edge of the driveway. The little one, a vision of cuteness in some sort of princess garb complete with tiara, fidgeted with her ponytail while the middle child, Amy now noticed, held pen and paper and wore yet another outfit—this time shorts and a top—covered in flowers.

The side door opened and a familiar-looking woman with spiky silver-colored hair peered out. Apparently Susan Wilson was fine.

"Girls, where are you?" she called

"Over here, Grammy," the little princess called. "With the lady who caught Skipper."

"The lady who…" She met Amy's stare. "Oh, my goodness. What is that dog doing out in the front yard?"

Amy smiled at the trim figure in white capri pants, sandals and a pale blue button-down shirt heading their way. "He was running toward the street with the girls close behind." She offered the dog's leash to the older woman. "I'm Amy," she said. "Amy Spencer. I work at the *Gazette*."

The grandmother gave Dr. Wilson's girls a look of relief before she turned her attention to Amy. "Pleased to meet you, Amy Spencer. I'm Susan Wilson and these are my granddaughters. This one's Ella. She'll be ten soon. Then comes eight-year-old Hailey."

"Hello, Ella and Hailey," Amy said when the eldest girl reached to shake her hand. Hailey offered a smile but made no move forward.

"And last but certainly not least," the vet's mother said, "this is Brooke. She just turned five and will start big-girl school in the fall." The little one rolled her eyes and tugged on her shorts. Apparently big-girl school was a sore subject for the youngest Wilson girl. "Say hello, Brooke," Mrs. Wilson urged.

The little one met Amy's gaze and grinned, showing a missing front tooth. "Hello," she said before ducking behind her grandmother. Amy returned the greeting when the girl peered out from under the older lady's arm.

"And of course, you've met Skipper." Susan Wilson's brown eyes twinkled. "I'd say the Lord had you in just the right spot this afternoon. Thank you for saving Skipper and the girls from what might have been a whole lot of trouble."

"You're welcome," Amy said quickly. "I'm glad I could help."

Behind her, the girls wore stricken looks. Obviously their grandmother had no idea a whole lot of trouble had already occurred.

Mrs. Wilson shook her head. "Tell me, Amy, how did you come to be standing in our driveway? I thought the girls had just phoned you to—" A car sped past and the dog made to follow. "Oh, no, you don't." When the car had safely disappeared around the corner, Mrs. Wilson turned the leash over to the eldest of the girls. "Ella, go on and take Skipper back inside the fence. Don't let him in the house just yet, though. I haven't finished cleaning up the remains of that platter he knocked off the counter."

"So that was what caused the crash I heard."

Mrs. Wilson returned her attention to Amy as the girls reluctantly hauled the Springer Spaniel back up the driveway. "I'm sorry?"

"Oh." Amy tucked a stray strand of hair behind her ear. "I was on the phone with the girls and I heard an awful noise that sounded like breaking glass. Of course, when I couldn't get an answer on the phone, I hurried over to check. You see, my grandmother fell a few months ago and…" She paused.

Had she said too much? Perhaps insinuated that Mrs. Wilson wasn't properly looking after her granddaughters?

The older woman crossed her arms over her chest and appeared to be considering something. Her smile settled Amy's concerns. "It takes a special person to find that level of concern for children." A pause. "And for me. I do appreciate what you've done today."

"I feel a little silly," Amy said. "And I'm terribly sorry for assuming."

"Don't you dare." The older woman waved away her concerns then winked. "So, did the girls manage to place the ad before the chaos began?" When Amy told her no, Mrs. Wilson's grin reappeared. "Come on inside and let me get my purse."

"Mrs. Wilson," Amy said carefully, "you do understand the girls were—"

"Playing matchmaker for their daddy?" Her smile broadened. "Yes, of course, dear. Who do you think dialed the phone for them? Now won't you come in and let me offer you some sweet tea and a slice of pie while I write a check for whatever this ad's going to cost?"

# Chapter Three

Amy shifted her purse off her shoulder then opened it to stuff her sunglasses inside. "Did I miss anything while I was gone?"

Bev swiveled around in her chair to give Amy her full attention. "Other than the earth-shattering news that the Vine Beach Washateria will be slashing their prices on the Sit and Spin special? No, nothing."

"Wow," Amy said with a half grin. "I'm going to miss working where the big news happens."

Shrugging, Bev pressed her glasses up a notch. "So, the classifieds emergency. How'd it turn out? Everything okay with the lady who wouldn't answer her phone?"

Amy groaned. "Turned out there was no emergency, after all. It was a misunderstanding. Though I did meet three adorable little girls and their grandmother. Oh, and their Springer Spaniel named Skipper. Whom I saved from running headlong into Elm Street. The girls had a little help in dialing the phone, and were calling to put an ad in the paper for a wife for their father. Not a girlfriend. Their father isn't interested in one of those. Their grandmother Susan thinks he's afraid to move on after his wife's death. So she paid for the ad, which will run in the next edition. I'm going to email her the receipt." She took a deep breath and exhaled slowly as she turned toward her cubicle. "All right, then. Back to the classifieds I go to watch the phone not ring."

"No, you don't." Bev followed Amy into her office and leaned against the door frame. In one hand she held a legal pad, and in the other, a pen. "You can't just leave me like that. I'm a reporter and this sounds like quite a story. Spill it, girl."

"Spill what?" Amy settled back into her chair.

"The dad. What's his name?"

Amy stowed her purse in the bottom drawer. "Dr. Eric Wilson."

"That yummy new vet?" She scribbled another note. "This just keeps getting better."

"Yes, that's the guy."

"Go on. Tell me everything from the beginning."

So she did, starting with the phone call and ending with the conversation she had over iced tea and peach pie with Susan Wilson, or "Grammy" as the girls called her. She did, however, skip the part where she'd spent a few minutes speaking to the vet in the park during her lunch hour. That, Amy decided, was off the record and definitely not pertinent to the story.

"I did get ad copy while I was there, but I'll work longer this evening to make up for the time I was gone," she added.

Bev waved away her statement. "You might not have realized it, but you *were* working, Amy. Even when you weren't getting ad copy."

"I was?"

"Yes, you were." She scanned her notes then

glanced back at Amy. "This is a great story. Definitely a human-interest angle."

"It is?"

"Plus, we haven't done anything on the new businesses in town in quite a while. What with Dr. Wilson taking over the practice, that's newsworthy in itself. Then there's the side story of his girls and their search for their new mama. All to draw attention to the ad, of course." She giggled. "Why, this is practically going to write itself. What did you say the name of the Cocker Spaniel is?"

"Skipper. And he's a Springer Spaniel." She peered over at Bev's notepad. "Are you really thinking about writing a story on this?"

"Why not?" Bev said. "Sure beats the article on the Sit and Spin special."

Amy laughed. "I suppose so."

"So, what does the ad say?"

Amy fished the paper from her purse. "'Best daddy in the world needs a wife. Must love dogs and little girls and sailboats and want to be married forever. Ask for Dr. Eric Wilson at Wilson Vet Clinic. Tell him Daddy's little matchmakers sent you.'" She paused to laugh at the memory of how long it took them to get the wording just right. "That's it. The girls came up with the ad and their grandmother paid for it. Susan assured me that Eric wouldn't mind the extra attention, what with the vet clinic being in need of new clients."

Bev nodded. "So this could be a PR stunt."

"I thought of that, actually," Amy said. "But if it is, the girls and their grandmother aren't showing any signs of it. They really appear to want Eric to find someone. Nothing more. I promise I asked a whole lot of questions before I agreed to take the ad."

"All right, then. I'll need a couple of quotes from you." She waited, pen poised.

"What kind of quotes?" Amy shook her head. "Hold that thought while I put my purse away."

"I'll get started on the article." Bev turned to head back down the hall. "Come into my office when you're done and we'll talk about it."

For all the interest this story might generate, it seemed a bit presumptuous to think this family might want this kind of publicity. In fact, given the tragedy surrounding Dr. Wilson's status as a widower, they might want just the opposite.

"Hey, Bev, do you really think this is worth writing about?" she called as she opened her desk drawer. "The Wilsons seem like nice people. And I haven't even spoken to Dr. Wilson." She paused to reconsider the statement. "At least not about the girls and this ad. Don't you want his side of the story? To make it more balanced?"

"No need," Bev called from around the corner. "He's well represented by his mother and daughters. Besides, it's the women's point of view that really makes this interesting, don't you think?"

"Well, okay," Amy said slowly as she found Bev's office and spied her jotting more notes on the almost-full page. "You're the reporter. But I'd hate to have their personal tragedy made so public."

Bev scribbled a second more then looked up. "Triumph over tragedy, Amy," she said. "That is definitely worth writing about. And I promise I'll be nice." She shrugged. "I've already got the headline all planned out. Daddy's Little Matchmakers."

\* \* \*

Eric Wilson slumped against the back of his chair and shook his head. "Mother, how in the world did they…"

Words escaped him. Between trying to make a success of the vet clinic and navigating the deep waters of grief over Christy's loss, he'd obviously found precious little time to attend to the needs of the girls. Why else would they have done something so ridiculous?

And of course they would find the one woman in town who didn't look at him as if he were the daily special at the Bachelor Buffet. He thought of Amy Spencer's easy smile and the way he enjoyed speaking to her earlier today and stifled a groan. What must she be thinking of him now? Had his girls really called her and caused a commotion?

"Hailey mentioned that you were considering putting the boat up for sale," his mother said, one brow lifted. "I assume one classified-ad idea led to another. Did you place yours?"

A shaft of guilt sliced at him. Perhaps he

should have mentioned something about parting with the boat before making the call.

"No, I was interrupted. I'm still considering it, actually." Eric gave his mother a level look. "But back to this ridiculous ad. Whose phone did the girls use?" he continued. "I haven't gotten around to putting in a home phone yet."

Eric watched a look he couldn't quite explain cross his mother's face. Slowly, she shrugged. "Does it matter?" He was about to answer when she continued. "By the way, Skipper got the remainder of the sandwiches so there'll be no leftovers." Mom chuckled. "You also need a new platter. He got that, too."

He groaned. What next?

"It's just about time to pick the girls up from ballet, so I should go. Please don't be too harsh with them tonight. They love you so." His mother reached for her car keys but made no further move to leave. "And by the way, Amy is a beautiful girl. Long blond curls and the loveliest eyes I've ever seen. No ring on her left hand, either."

"Mother, seriously." He leaned forward to rest his elbows on his desk and sighed. Even now the gaping wound of Christy's death felt fresh. "You know I'm not interested in dating anyone. It's just too soon, no matter what my daughters seem to think."

"Son," his mother said gently, "it's been almost four years. Christy would never have wanted you to grieve so long when—"

"I can count." Eric exhaled slowly and pinched the bridge of his nose. "Look, I'm sorry. Coming here to take over Doc Simmons's practice was a good move. I'll never doubt the Lord led us to Vine Beach, and I know the girls love being back here so close to you. So do I."

"And you know it's an answered prayer for me, dear. This grandma's heart was breaking with you and those girls so far away."

Eric exhaled slowly. Leaving the home in Dallas that he'd shared with Christy had been the hardest thing he'd done since the funeral. And yet it did feel good to be with people who didn't constantly ask him how he was doing.

"While I'm sure you're right about why the girls and I are here, I'm also certain His immediate purpose was not to make me wealthy." He gave his mother a second to take that in. "So, yes, I did have the paper open to the classifieds section. I figured what I could get from the sailboat would cover the bills for a few months. That ought to give God enough time to do a miracle."

To Eric's surprise, his mother actually laughed. "Sweetheart, do you think God needs your help doing anything, miracles or otherwise?"

"I suppose not." His vet tech knocked then slid the door open to indicate his next patient had arrived. "But while I'm waiting for Him, the bills won't wait for me."

"All right." Mom stood and clutched her purse. "But might I suggest you pray about selling that boat? I can't help but think God has another way of filling this need."

"I already have," Eric said. "I suppose if He wants me to keep the boat, He'll handle the details."

"Oh, He's certainly in the detail-handling business," she said. "And just one more suggestion before I let you get back to work."

"All right." Eric pushed a button to activate the speakerphone then set the receiver back on the cradle and rose to reach for his lab coat.

"Your daughters didn't call the classifieds for no reason, Eric. Amy told me they were quite specific. They wanted a wife for you, not a girlfriend. Said you weren't interested in girlfriends. Wonder where they heard that? The comment about girlfriends, I mean."

How many times had he responded to his girls' pleas with that statement? And yet even now Eric could testify to the truth of it. The last thing he needed right now was a romantic relationship causing further complications in his life. If only his mother and daughters would understand this.

"Eric, look at me." When he complied, Mother's expression softened. "Honey, you need to let this go." Before he could protest, her grip tightened again. "I mean it, Eric. And don't tell me I have no idea what you're talking about because I do. I lost my spouse, too. Not in the same way as you, but I do know what it is to lose the one you love, and you know it."

He did. Eric nodded and covered his mother's hand with his own.

"So let me give you some unsolicited advice. If you don't get out there and start living again, you're going to die inside and have nothing to offer anyone. Not your daughters or me or anyone else. Is that what you want?" She released her grip to wrap her arms around her waist. "Is this what Christy would have wanted?"

Eric's temper sparked. "That's not fair, Mother. You cannot know what she would have wanted, and I'd appreciate it if you didn't bother to try."

"Yes, I can, Eric, and so can you. She told you she didn't want you to grieve her."

His heart thudded against his chest. "How did you know?"

"Because she told me," his mother said gently. "She knew you wouldn't listen to her, I suppose. Or maybe she wanted me to be sure of it. Anyway, Christy loved you enough to ask that you get on with your life in her memory. And that her memory didn't consume you. She lives on through those girls, Eric. But are you really living?"

"I am," he said with more than a little irritation in his voice.

Her expression softened. "No, sweetheart,"

she said as her eyes misted with unshed tears, "you're not."

"Mom," he said as he gathered her into an embrace. "Don't. I'll get this figured out. I promise." He held her a moment longer then patted her back and held her at arm's length. "For the girls' sake, I will."

She nodded, her eyes shining. "Would you do one more thing for me?" At Eric's skeptical glance, his mother continued. "Hold off on selling the boat. At least for a little while. You all loved sailing, and I'd hate to see it go."

"I would hate to see it go, as well, but I'll do what I have to do to provide for my family." He paused only long enough to offer his mother a smile. "However, I haven't placed the ad yet."

"And I hope you don't have to." She held up her hand to wave off any response from him. "But before any of that, you still need to speak to your daughters."

"I plan to, Mother," he said wearily.

"Promise?"

"Yes, I promise. Right after I call the *Gazette* to stop the ad then ground the girls for using your cell phone without permission."

"It's too late to call. The paper closes at four. And who said they didn't have permission, Eric?" she said as she slipped out into the hall.

"Mother, come back here," he called as he started to follow her.

"Sorry, darling," his mother said sweetly as she waved over her shoulder. "The girls will be wondering where I am, and you've got patients to see."

He cast a glance at his watch and then back at the lone file on his desk. "Patient," Eric corrected under his breath. "At least I'll be home early tonight, and I can sleep late."

This thought kept him going through the remainder of the afternoon and got him through the bedtime routine that sometimes derailed his patience. Tonight, however, the older two girls were unusually compliant, taking their baths and climbing under the covers without a single complaint.

That in itself was suspicious. But when Brooke, the baby girl who was growing up far too fast, kissed him good-night and marched off to bed without a single request for water or a second story to be read, Eric suspected something was up.

He loaded the supper dishes into the dishwasher and reset the coffeepot for tomorrow then waited a full five minutes longer before tiptoeing down the hall to see if he could catch the trio at whatever trouble they'd planned. Instead, he found his girls sound asleep, bathed in the pale yellow glow of the night-light.

Eric padded back to the kitchen and turned off the lights. Standing in the darkened room, he closed his eyes and inhaled deeply of the spice-scented candle his mother insisted made a suitable centerpiece for the table. What she couldn't have known is the smell reminded him of Christy. Cinnamon and spice had always been her favorite scent.

Opening his eyes, Eric scooped the candle off the table and marched outside. The warm night air fell around him like a salt-tinged blanket as he walked barefoot to the trash can behind the garage. Lifting the lid, he hesitated only a moment before throwing the candle into the deep recesses of the empty can then slamming the lid back down tightly.

He returned inside and fell into the recliner. Reaching for the remote, Eric turned on the television but after realizing he'd heard nothing of what the talking head on the sports channel had said, he shut off the television and went to bed.

Tomorrow would be another day, he reminded himself as his head hit the pillow. Fridays were generally slow at the clinic—slower than even the snail's pace of the other weekdays—so he'd decided starting today he wouldn't go in until noon unless there was an emergency.

Maybe he'd set the alarm and make pancakes. Eric smiled. Yes, pancakes. A reward for the girls' good behavior in going to bed so nicely. And just maybe, a chance to see what in the world they were up to. Also, a way to have a nice family meeting regarding why they would not be placing any more ads.

"The ad." Eric scribbled a note to remind himself to call the *Gazette* first thing. Perhaps he could stop the ad before it went to print.

After a fitful night of mostly missed sleep, Eric rolled over and reached for his phone as soon as the alarm went off. "Classifieds, please," he said when the call was answered.

"I'm sorry, there's no one in yet. May I take a message?"

Stifling a yawn, Eric laid back against the pillows. "Yes, please. This is for Amy Spencer or whoever has the power to pull an ad before it goes to press. Please call Eric Wilson at—"

"*The* Eric Wilson? From Daddy's Little Matchmakers?"

He groaned. "Yes."

"What a great story. We've already had inquiries on it."

Sitting bolt upright, Eric gripped the phone. "Wait. You're saying the ad has already gone to print? But it was just placed yesterday afternoon. I thought there was a lag time of a day or two. Your paper only comes out once a week."

"All the more reason to get such a great story in quickly," the woman said with a lilt in her voice. "Was there anything else I could help you with?"

"No, nothing," he managed.

"Amy's last day was yesterday but I'm sure someone can call you back if you'd like. I'll have to check and see who's handling classifieds now that the temp job is finished. Would you like me to do that?"

"No," he snapped. "I don't think that would

be a good idea. But you could do me one favor."

"What's that, Dr. Wilson?"

"Could you tell whoever's inquiring that there's no story here? Its just three little girls and one nosy grandmother trying to run my life. I love them but I certainly don't want to encourage them."

A giggle and then she said, "Can I quote you on that, Dr. Wilson?"

"No," he said a bit too harshly before hanging up.

Later that morning Eric scooped the last pancake off the griddle and added it to the stack. With summer upon them, that meant he could spend the morning with the girls before his mother came to take up her babysitting duties. Even as he grumbled over the embarrassment of the ad, he gave a quick thanks for Mom—whose home was a short three blocks away—as he reached into the pantry for the syrup. Maple for Ella and Hailey, and strawberry for Brooke.

"Girls," he called as he said a prayer for guidance before their family meeting. "Breakfast."

Down the hall they came, a scampering herd of pink-clad girls whose giggles and squeals were forever imprinted on his heart. One by one he greeted them and then, with a great show of mock formality, he set their glasses of juice and milk before them.

"Look, Daddy's using the stick glasses."

Hailey lifted the glass, a piece of wedding crystal that had been woefully hidden away for special occasions—until this last move. Since Christy's death, Eric had learned that any day he woke up and put both feet on the floor was a special occasion.

He slid his Bible out of the way and sat the milk carton on the counter. Tucked into the pages of the well-worn book was a neon-green flyer for Starting Over—the new men's group for widowers that the church advertised last Sunday.

Wincing, Eric recalled sitting through the clever basketball-themed video the pastor had shown last Sunday. While he loved the sport, the idea of getting together with a bunch of guys on Saturday morning to shoot hoops and talk about their grief certainly did not appeal.

And even if it did, Saturday mornings were always spent with the girls.

It was their time, and nothing would come between him and his girls. Not even a group that purported to offer help to men stuck in the cycle of grief. If the Lord wanted him at that group, He'd just have to clear the time.

Which Eric knew He wouldn't.

So he turned his back on the thought and joined the girls at the table. He was doing just fine, and anyone who told him otherwise was just wrong.

"Look, Daddy, my pancakes are pink."

Eric glanced over at Brooke's plate and found she'd mixed her milk with the syrup to form a gooey glob of her favorite color. "Nice, Brookie" was all he could manage. No sense in correcting what could become a budding culinary career. "Now tell me how pink tastes."

"Daddy, Hailey's making flowers with the syrup again."

A glance at his middle daughter's plate confirmed Ella's complaint. Rather than pour syrup over her pancakes, his artistic child was making elaborate swirls and tiny leaves to decorate what was a garden of floral delights. All while her older sister waited for her turn at the syrup bottle.

"I'm just getting it right, Daddy," she said. "I don't want to mess up the flowers."

"Enough, Hailey," Eric said. "Let Ella have—" His cell phone rang, and Eric debated a moment before he reached for it. The clinic. "Dr. Wilson," he said as he rose to step away from the now-chattering females.

"Hey, Doc," his receptionist said. "Things have gotten kind of busy and it might be a good idea if you come in earlier than you planned."

Skipper came bounding in the dog door shaking his wet coat all over the cabinets, the walls and the newly refinished wood floor. "Sure, soon as I talk to the girls and clean up this mess," he said as he hurried to end the call.

A glance around the room told Eric that the conversation with the girls would have to wait until tonight. Cleaning up the dog's mess soon turned into cleaning up the girls' mess and then, after that, to turning on the sprinklers in the backyard and creating a make-do

Slip'n Slide out of the leftover plastic tarps the painters left behind. By the time his mother arrived, Eric was covered in pieces of grass and soaked head to toe.

"Well, now," she said as she wisely stood out of the range of the girls' splashes. "Is this any way for the town's most eligible bachelor to behave?"

"Mother, really." He grabbed a towel off the fence and began to dry off. "Not in front of the girls."

"What do you mean 'not in front of the girls'?"

"I mean we're having a good time." He looked back to note three sets of eyes staring in their direction. "So leave off with the eligible-bachelor stuff, okay?" he added in a much quieter voice.

"They look awfully happy. You didn't punish them, did you?" She gave him one of those "Mom" looks.

"Actually I haven't had a chance to speak to them." He shook his head. "But no, they won't be punished. Not since they had you egging them on."

His mother lifted a silver brow. "Egging

them on? Really, Eric, you act as if I'm the only one who wants you to find someone to love."

"Grammy, come swim with us," Brooke called.

"Grammy didn't bring her suit," she said as she glanced over her shoulder. "Maybe tomorrow morning I can take you all to the pool at the community center. Or maybe to the beach. If it's all right with your daddy." His mother turned her attention to Eric. "You didn't have anything planned for tomorrow morning, did you?"

"Tomorrow morning?" His heart sank. "No," he replied weakly. "Just spending time with the girls like we do every Saturday. I suppose we could go to the pool."

"Looks like you just spent the morning with them, Eric." Mom gave him her most radiant grin. "And no offense, but I was hoping to make this a girls-only morning. Maybe go get our nails done and our toes painted afterward. Is that awful?"

"No, it's fine," he said as three girls began to cheer. "Great." His mother clapped her hands. "I had hoped to take them to breakfast, too.

So, I'll be here around seven-thirty. Is that too early?"

"Too early? No, I don't suppose." Especially since the men's group meeting began at eight.

"Well, go on and get ready for work, then," she said brightly as Hailey called for her. "Grammy's got it covered out here."

Eric reluctantly complied, grumbling his way through his shower, getting dressed and then making the short commute to the clinic. As was his custom, he pulled around to the back only to find there were no empty parking spaces.

"That's strange," he said as he drove around to the front of the building only to see the parking spaces on Main Street filled, as well. Across the way, the *Gazette*'s parking lot was also at capacity. "Must be a sale going on over at the shoe store."

He finally found a parking spot down at the Vine Beach Public Library some three blocks away. By the time Eric reached the front door, the Texas sun had begun to toast the back of his neck and his shirt was soaked. He was, quite literally, hot under the collar and beginning to steam.

Before he could wrap his fingers around the knob, the door flew open. "Thank goodness you're here, Doc," his receptionist said. "I didn't have a clue what to do with all the calls for appointments."

"Appointments?" Eric walked in to find the tiny office filled with pets and their owners, the great majority of whom were women. All chairs were occupied and a woman in tight jeans holding a mewling cat in a hot-pink cage leaned against the opposite wall.

"Hello, Eric," she said when she met his gaze.

Eric? He nodded in greeting then stepped around her. The phones were ringing and the crowd at the front desk was three deep. A teacup Chihuahua shivered violently, it's diamond-studded collar sending rainbow sparks across the worn floorboards while a Yorkie with blue hair bows relieved herself behind the lone plant.

Nancy, his vet tech, was pulling files and adding them to a thick stack. Rather than working in the back at her grooming table, Cassie Jo seemed to be busy printing what appeared to be new-client forms. Dee had one phone to her ear and another resting in the crook of her arm. It was not immediately apparent whether she was speaking to the caller or the dark-haired matron at the front of the line.

"Follow me," Eric said to Nancy as he stepped over a pet carrier and hurried to the solitude of his office. "All right," he said when she shut the door behind her. "What's going on?"

Her smile was inappropriate to the stress of the situation. "My guess is they're all here to see you."

"Me?" Eric shook his head. "I don't know what's going on here." He took a deep breath and let it out slowly. "Look," he said with what he hoped would be a calmer voice, "I know you don't know me all that well, but I'm usually a guy who can laugh right along with the rest of them. The catch is, I need to be in on the joke. So, why don't you tell all those people to go home so I can have my parking place and my office back?"

Nancy gestured to the folded copy of the *Gazette* that topped the stack of periodicals on the corner of his desk. "See for yourself." She paused. "You might want to sit down."

"Surely all of this insanity wasn't caused by that ridiculous ad in the classifieds. Who reads that section, anyway?"

His vet tech shook her head. "Don't know about that but I'm pretty sure everyone reads the headlines." She shrugged. "See for yourself. If you don't need me for anything else, though, I probably should get out there and help."

"No, go ahead." He waited until Nancy left then carefully opened the paper to read the headline. "Daddy's Little Matchmakers."

Before he could read past the first paragraph, the intercom buzzed. "Yes?"

"Phone's for you, hon," the receptionist said. "And you'll probably want to take this one."

"What?" He shook his head. "Not right now."

"No, seriously," she repeated. "You want to take this."

Eric leaned back, exasperated. "And why would that be?" he managed.

"Well, it's some reporter from the *Houston Chronicle*. Said she read the most interesting story about you on the newswire this morning. Wants to know if you have any comments she can put in the story she's writing."

"Great," he said weakly.

"Line three." Nancy's voice dissolved into a giggle as she skittered out of the room and left him alone with the red light blinking on line three and a *Houston Chronicle* reporter asking for details of his search for a bride.

# Chapter Four

❧

Friday afternoon ended with Amy bolting out of the empty house on Vine Street and heading toward the beach. Knee-deep in the warm Gulf, she lost herself in the swirling waters she loved so much.

A steady line of traffic moved down Vine Street, passing silently between her and Nana's white cottage. From her vantage point she could see the swing swaying gently beneath the arbor of sunny yellow Lady Banks roses. And while the white picket fence hid them, Amy knew the blossoms in Nana's perennial garden were swaying, as well, though the weeds around them were likely moving in unison.

She turned her face to the salt-tinged wind.

Something about the topography of the land and the angle of the waves kept a breeze blowing year-round at Vine Beach. At least that's how Grandpa had tried to explain the phenomenon, though she'd never known whether a bit of his theory was true. Her stomach growled, a reminder that she'd only snacked on cheese and crackers for lunch.

Tucking an errant curl behind her ear, Amy was swishing through the water toward the sandy shore when her cell phone began to ring. A quick glance at the display told her that the temp agency was on the other end of the line.

Her heart sank. Just yesterday upon completion of her assignment at the *Gazette,* the agency's administrator had told her that there was no more work for her in Vine Beach. All taken by summer workers willing to take minimum wage, she'd been told. While the news had been delivered in an apologetic tone, Amy had felt as if a weight had been lifted.

If a job had been found, she might have to rethink her theory that lack of work meant it was time to leave Vine Beach. Amy said a quick prayer that this would not be the case.

"Hello," she said on the third ring.

"Amy, I'm so glad I caught you before the end of the day," the agency administrator said. "There's been an opening for an assistant at Dr. Wilson's clinic. He's specifically asked for you. Monday morning. Seven a.m. sharp. No idea of how long he'll need you, so this one's open-ended. Might become permanent."

Her breath caught and for a moment, Amy considered the proposition of working for the vet. Then clarity and good sense told her what to say. With no idea of what she was supposed to do next, it was not the time to take on another temp job. At least not one that might become permanent. No need to leave him one employee short should she decide to leave town.

"No, I'm not interested, but please tell Dr. Wilson thank you."

"Are you certain?"

"I am," Amy quickly replied. "I'm really not sure how much longer I'll be in Vine Beach, so I can't really commit to another job right now."

"I'll let him know."

Amy hung up with a promise to update her contact information should she decide to leave town. Replacing the phone in her pocket, Amy shook her head. Why in the world would Eric Wilson specifically ask for her? Very odd indeed.

Perhaps she should call Dr. Wilson and explain her reason for declining his offer. Then she might also have to answer for why she contributed to the story that landed in today's headlines.

She went to bed still debating the issue and awoke to decide that weeding the gardens was a much better idea than taking on such a task. Thus, Amy spent Saturday morning tending to the long-overdue chore of caring for her grandmother's garden. While she worked, her mind once again wandered back to what Eric Wilson might think about the article in the *Gazette*. Surely he would understand that she'd only performed the duties of her job. That anyone who happened to answer the phone would have done the same.

And there could have been something seriously wrong with his mother.

"Who am I kidding? If it were me, I'd be

horrified," Amy muttered as she swiped at the perspiration on her brow. "I should have minded my own business. And I certainly shouldn't have said anything to Bev."

The article hadn't been all that awful. A little embarrassing if you were of a mind to prefer your privacy, but not awful.

Shrugging off the thought, Amy leaned back on her heels and sighed. More pressing was the fact that as of yesterday, nothing held her in Vine Beach other than the silly notion that her grandmother might eventually come to need her again.

She wouldn't, of course, at least not anytime soon. Rather, since moving into the assisted-living facility, her grandmother's social life had blossomed, and with it any question of her return to the cottage on Vine Beach disappeared. The issue now was what to do with the house. And what to do with herself. For much as she loved to sit on the swing and stare across Vine Street at the gray-green water of the Gulf of Mexico, Amy knew the situation was only temporary.

When she took the three-month assignment at the *Gazette,* Amy promised herself when the work there was done she would make plans to move on. Three months had seemed like a very long time when she took on the commitment. Now that she'd seen the assignment to its completion, she felt no closer to knowing what came next.

Perhaps she'd go back home to Houston and return to the flower shop. Unfortunately, every time she thought to broach the subject with Mom or Dad, she found it impossible to do so. The words just wouldn't come out. Finally Amy realized that much as she loved her parents, the Lord seemed to be leading her elsewhere. But where? So far He'd been silent on that.

So, she'd filled out a few applications last night online and printed out her résumé to mail three more. If the Lord wanted her here, He wouldn't allow any of those inquiries to become offers.

At least she knew she'd done something. Anything. Now she could only wait.

She straightened and gathered up the basket, the summer sun warm on her shoulders. Across Vine Street, the sound of waves breaking on Vine Beach beckoned. Amy cast a glance around the vegetable garden with a satisfied smile. The morning's work had been productive, and she'd picked enough to make a nice salad for lunch.

Porch salad. Amy smiled as she thought of the name she and her grandmother had given to the salads made from the garden. Whatever they picked they washed and chopped into a mishmash of vegetables that were served up on Nana's porch in bowls taken from the cabinet in the dining room. Something about the combination of the rose-covered fancy china, the lace tablecloth cast over the old wicker table at the corner of the porch and the best view of the Gulf of Mexico on all of Vine Street made each porch salad meal unforgettable.

She shook off the dirt from her gloves then gathered up the basket and strolled toward the back door. Just inside the kitchen, after leaving her gloves and shoes outside, an idea occurred, and Amy reached for her phone to call her grandmother. Why have porch salad alone?

"Sweetie, much as I would love a good porch salad, you know it's my bingo day and we always have lunch together after," Nana said once the pleasantries were exchanged and Amy's purpose for calling divulged.

"Is it?" she asked as she retrieved the colander and sat it in the sink to begin rinsing the vegetables.

After a long pause, Nana said, "Amy girl, are you all right?"

She turned her back to the sink and leaned against the counter, one arm around her waist. On the opposite wall, the old regulator clock ticked a comforting, even rhythm.

"I'm fine, Nana," she said as brightly as she could manage.

"How's that job going down at the paper? Goodness but today's headline about those darling little girls was something."

"The job ended yesterday, actually, and the headline…" She paused to reach behind her and turn off the water. "It certainly was something."

"I know Susan Wilson must be tickled pink that Eric's finally going to get over his loss. I need to call her. Yes, I'll do that right after bingo."

She froze. "You know Mrs. Wilson?"

"Of course I do," Nana said. "Known her for years. I believe we first met at the Garden Club meetings. Or maybe it was volunteering over at the old folks' home. Before we were both old folks, of course. Anyway, she's got an absolutely green thumb when it comes to roses. No one grows them as thick and pretty as Susie." A pause while she chuckled. "Except me, of course. But then, I taught her everything she knows."

While Nana rambled on about soil enhancements and the benefits of deadheading roses earlier rather than later in the season, Amy moved to the tiny kitchen table and sat down. From her vantage point, she could see the climbing rose on the trellis that Grandpa had built so long ago. In another month, the sturdy vine would be covered in a profusion of pink blooms.

A pity she wouldn't be here. She would have to arrange with someone at the assisted-living facility to bring Nana out to see them.

"Sweetheart," her grandmother said, "you're a dear for letting me go on about roses and such, but I am afraid I'm going to have to hang up. It's just about bingo time and I haven't done a thing with my hair yet."

"Of course. Have a great time with the ladies, Nana," she said.

"I will, sweetie," she said. "Oh, wait. Listen to me going on about flowers and bingo when I didn't even think to ask what you're going to do next."

"Next?"

"Yes, you said you were finished with your job at the paper. What will you do next?"

Amy leaned back in the chair and thought of yesterday's call from the temp agency. "I don't know, Nana. I had thought once I was finished at the *Gazette,* I might…"

"You might what?"

"Oh, I don't know. I guess I just never thought that I was supposed to live in Vine Beach permanently."

There. She'd said it. Aloud. Amy held her breath and waited for Nana's response.

"Well, of course you didn't," her grandmother said lightly. "You came for me and now that I'm on the mend, you've got to decide what the Lord's asking of you next."

"Yes," she said on an exhale of breath. "That's it exactly."

"So what's He telling you, sweetie?"

"That's the problem," Amy admitted as she rose and moved down the hall toward the front door. "I keep asking, and I even sent out a few job inquiries, but so far He hasn't responded and neither have the employers."

"Yes, He has," Nana said. "Surely you understand that no response is also an answer."

Amy stood at the front door looking through its beveled glass to the beach and the shimmering water beyond. "I suppose," she said. "But what I don't understand is what I do about it."

"It?"

"Staying in Vine Beach," she said. "What's God telling me about that?"

"In my experience when God isn't telling you to do something new, He means for you to keep doing the last thing He told you to do."

"Nana, I don't even remember what that was," she said as she saw a familiar truck pull into the driveway and stop.

"Sure you do, sweetie," Nana said. "He told you to come to Vine Beach. Well, here you are and I suppose it's here you stay until He says otherwise."

"Yes, well, enjoy your day," Amy said as she watched Eric Wilson climb out of the truck.

Eric slammed the truck door then took a deep breath and let it out slowly. Coming here was a bad idea. But then so had going to the church support group for widowers. He'd managed to get all the way into the parking lot before good sense prevailed and he drove back home.

Back home, he'd found the quiet—brought on by his mother's insistence on having a girls' day with his daughters—impossible to bear. So he'd gone to work.

Another mistake, for the moment he drove into the parking lot, he was set upon by a woman who had hoped he kept office hours on Saturday. Suspiciously, she carried not a pet but a copy of yesterday's *Gazette.*

That had sent Eric hurrying back to his truck. And somehow between Main Street and Vine Street, he'd decided to speak to Amy Spencer personally about the current state of his life. At least the part that was her fault.

He'd circled the block three times. Finding out where Amy Spencer lived had been easy, given the size of Vine Beach and his mother's propensity to talk about who was related to whom.

Before he could change his mind again, Eric bounded toward the front steps of the picturesque home then stopped short of his destination when the door opened and Amy Spencer stepped out onto the porch. His gaze collided with blue eyes the color of the afternoon sky, and the speech he prepared—where he told her exactly how he felt about her part in everything from the humiliating headline to the near mutiny his office staff staged yesterday afternoon—completely evaporated.

Unlike her professional appearance yesterday, the classifieds girl's curls had been captured in a somewhat messy knot at the nape of her neck, leaving her shoulders bare beneath the pale pink floral sundress. As the screen door slammed behind her, Amy's eyes narrowed.

He hadn't thought of it until just now, but Christy's eyes had also been blue. Eric saw them every day in his daughter's faces. But unlike the color of soft denim that his late wife had handed down to the girls, Amy Spencer's eyes were the startling pale shade of robin's eggs.

Eric expected she might speak first, and truly she appeared to consider it. When the silence stretched too long, he said, "I guess you're wondering why I'm here."

She worried with a small heart-shaped locket, strung on a thin gold chain at her neck. "If it's about the job…"

Leaning against the rail, Eric felt the worn wood sway slightly. A quick look told him it could use a coat of paint, as well. Signs of a lack of attention that could easily be remedied. He forced his attention back on Miss Spencer. "The agency told me you turned my job offer down."

"I did."

Eric waited for an explanation, one that was obviously not forthcoming. "Any reason?" he finally asked. "I thought the salary was generous, and I can guarantee there will be plenty to keep you busy."

*Thanks to you and your snooping,* he wanted to say.

"Yes, actually." She stopped toying with the locket and allowed her hand to fall to her side. "I'm leaving Vine Beach soon."

The news hit him with an unexpected stab of disappointment. And then he recalled just how much trouble Amy Spencer could pack into a short time.

"Soon as in when?" he said. "Because thanks to a certain article in the local paper, my office is swamped with women whose pets don't have a thing wrong with them beyond the fact their owners are single. And my office staff? I've gone from wondering how I will pay the women I inherited from the vet who retired to wondering how I can keep them from quitting. So if you're still here on Monday morning, I think it would be a good idea for you to come and help fix what you've caused."

"Fix what I've caused?" She shook her head. "Look, I'm sorry for any trouble the newspaper article caused but I assure you it was not my intention."

His patience snapped. "A reporter from the *Houston Chronicle* called yesterday, and my office manager told me she's fielded phone calls from a half-dozen television stations in a four-state area as well as CNN and Fox News. And every one of them wants to know about my search for a wife. For a *wife,*" he repeated before taking a deep breath. "And never mind the fact I'm trying to figure out how to tell my daughters they've done something wrong without breaking their hearts. I'd call that trouble whether you intended it or not," Eric managed in a calmer tone.

Color rose in Amy's face, belying the cool breeze that danced through her curls. "I did not ask to be any part of this, Dr. Wilson. Your daughters called me."

"They are children," he said, though he suspected those children had more than a little help from his mother. How much help he'd yet to pry out of her. "And you are an adult."

"As is your mother," she said evenly.

That reminder caused him to pause a moment. "While I'm sure they were only trying to help me," he said after a moment, "I can't say that I believe that's what you were thinking."

"Oh, really?" The former classifieds girl straightened her spine and eyed him as if he were the most distasteful thing she'd seen all day. "What is it you believe I was thinking?"

"I believe you were asking yourself how you could get out of the classifieds department and into the big time as a real reporter. And along came my three girls. Bam! You had your story."

"And I planned all that?" Sarcasm seeped from her words. "Really?"

Logic took a little of the bluster from his response. "No," he said slowly as he struggled to think on the fly, "but you seized the opportunity when it was presented to you."

"Seized the opportunity," she echoed. "That's an interesting theory, Dr. Wilson. But if I'm so interested to rise to the coveted ranks of reporter at the *Gazette,* explain to me why not only do I no longer work there as of Thursday at 4:00 p.m., but I am also planning to leave Vine Beach." A pause, punctuated by a triumphant stare. "How do you explain that?"

He picked at a flake of white paint on the stair rail then sent her a look. "I'd explain it by saying you got a better offer. My guess is Houston or Dallas."

Her laughter caught him by surprise. "I hope you're better at diagnosing animals than you are at figuring out people."

Eric had no response for that. A passing car honked and Eric turned to see Riley Burkett, a friend he'd met at church. He returned Riley's wave then looked once again at Amy Spencer.

"So, you're not as quick to speak now?" she said.

"I've said enough." He stuffed his hands in the pockets of his jeans. "And I stand by what I said."

"Then you'll be surprised to know that I am a florist by trade, not a reporter, and I have no intention of having anything to do with a newspaper of any kind other than reading one on occasion. I came to Vine Beach to take care of my grandmother after her fall." Her expression sobered. "I thought your mother had fallen. That's how all this started."

Her statement took Eric aback. "What are you talking about?"

She gave him a pointed look. "When the girls called, I thought it was a prank call. I worked in classifieds three months. You'd be surprised at what people think is funny."

Rather than respond, Eric remained silent.

"The call came in while I was out at lunch." She paused. "Talking to you in the park, actually." Amy appeared to let the statement sink in a moment before continuing. "So when I got back to my desk, there was the sweetest message. I returned the call. Your mother answered, and she passed the phone on to one of the girls. All three of them, actually, but anyway, before we could complete the wording of the ad, there was a crash and some noise that sounded like breaking glass. Then the screaming. And there was barking, which I now know belonged to Skipper. The dog."

"Yes, I know my own dog's name," he snapped. "Sorry. You were saying."

"The line disconnected, and when I tried to call back no one answered. I assumed…"

Realization dawned. "You assumed my mother had fallen."

Her nod was almost imperceptible. "No one was there when my grandmother fell. She lay there for hours until…"

An image that didn't quite fit his idea of who Amy Spencer was rose in his mind. Until now he'd imagined she'd gone to his home in search of a story.

"Anyway," she continued, "as it turns out, the dog knocked a platter of sandwiches off the counter. That was the cause of the sound of breaking glass as well as all the other noise. And lest you think your mom was being negligent, she told me she was just outside the back door watering her roses."

Eric took a deep breath and let it out slowly. "Then I owe you an apology. For being wrong about why you went to my home." He held up his hand to silence her response. "However, the fact remains that you sold my daughters and me up the river with that article, and now my office is full of women thinking they want to be the next Mrs. Wilson."

Laughter again, this time with much more humor in it. "Isn't that what the girls wanted?"

"The girls don't get to decide."

His statement made her look away. "I guess you're right." She returned her attention to him. "But for the record, I never set out to see your story in print. I had to let someone know where I was going when I left to check on your mom. So I told Bev."

"The reporter."

"Yes, but only because she was the only other person in the office, and I had to tell someone why I was leaving during office hours when I'd only just returned from lunch. When I got back, she wanted to know what happened. So I told her."

Much as he hated to admit it, the woman made sense. Still, he was left with a staff that would stage a walkout on Monday morning if he didn't provide someone to help them with the increased patient load.

"When she said it would make a great human-interest piece," Amy continued, "I… well, I guess I've just got a weak spot for happily-ever-after stories, and it sounded like you were due one."

That took the wind out of his sails. Eric searched for a response and found he had none.

Amy shifted positions and looked past him, presumably to the beach or the ocean beyond. "There's something I'm a little confused about. If you were that bothered by my part in this article, why ask the temp agency specifically for me?"

This he could answer. "My staff has threatened to walk out on Monday morning if I don't provide them with help in dealing with the influx of patients. I don't blame them. However, who better to help solve a problem than the person who created it?"

Amy's attention jerked back to him. "That's not fair. Bev's the one who thought…" She shook her head. "I see what you mean. But how did you know I was available to hire? I don't recall telling you that I worked for the temp agency, and I know I didn't tell you that I no longer worked at the paper."

"That was easy," he said. "There's only one temp agency in town. When I called to see who was available on short notice, I was told I could have my choice of several high-school students who would be available to start summer jobs next week, or I could hire you. I specifically asked for you." Eric paused to give her an appraising look. "I figured there was some sort of poetic justice in that."

"Poetic justice," she echoed. "Yes, I suppose so. But as I've told you, I have no experience working in a veterinary clinic. I'm a florist who happens to know how to answer the phone and type."

"Can't see the need for any flower arranging on this job," Eric said, "but if you can type, file things alphabetically and answer the phone, you're overqualified." He paused. "That is, if you're not leaving town immediately."

She looked surprised, then by degrees Amy began to smile. "I suppose I could fill in for a few days."

"That would be great." He reached to shake her hand. "A few days are a good start. At least I won't have to hire a whole new staff on Tuesday," he called over his shoulder on his way to the truck. "See you Monday morning at seven sharp."

Eric climbed into the truck and jabbed his keys into the ignition. As the motor roared to life, he sat back against the seat and watched Amy Spencer disappear inside. "Amy?" he called before the screen door had shut completely.

She stepped back outside. "What is it?"

"Thank you," he said.

"You might want to hold your gratitude until you see what sort of help I'll actually be."

# Chapter Five

Amy had told the truth when she said she had no qualifications for working in a vet's office. He'd excused her first day on the job, memorable for her enthusiasm and mistakes offered in equal measure, and had tried to remind himself that her second day on the job was part of the learning curve. But today, when despite her best efforts to the contrary, she'd managed to dismantle the copier, jam the printer and accidentally shred the records of three active patients all before noon, Eric was ready to fire her.

"Don't you dare," Nancy said when he announced at the regular Wednesday lunchtime staff meeting—which he'd not mentioned to

Amy—that their newest employee was about to go. "Amy's great."

"Amy is not great," Eric argued. "Look at the havoc she's caused." He turned his attention to the groomer. "Cassie Jo, didn't you just tell me yesterday afternoon that she put the wrong collar on Mrs. Wyatt's Pomeranian?"

Cassie Jo shifted positions and nodded with a toss of her ponytail. "That's true. But she's also the only one who could brush that dog's teeth without getting bit. I'd say that's a fair trade."

His vet tech agreed and then the receptionist chimed in, and before long all three women were extolling the wonder that was Amy Spencer. Finally Eric had heard enough.

"Hold on here," he said. "Are you saying that even though she's made mistake after mistake, I should keep her? I thought the point of hiring someone to help was that they would actually help."

"She can type," Dee offered.

"When she manages to find the correct file," Eric countered.

"And she's great with the owners." This from the groomer. "I don't have to worry about whether someone's going to complain about how the dog comes out because even the grumpy owners leave smiling. And you should see how well she handles the PMWs."

Eric held up his hand. "Wait a minute. The PMWs?"

"The Prospective Mrs. Wilsons," Dee said. "There've been so many calls we had to come up with a separate category when we're scheduling appointments."

"Or rather not scheduling them," Nancy said.

"Unless they're really sweet or someone we know."

The other two nodded, leaving Eric completely astounded. And temporarily speechless.

Rather than continue to support his unpopular position, he chose to wave off any further comments and dismiss the meeting. As they we were filing out, however, Eric called them back.

"Here's the deal," he told them. "If you want Amy to stay, you're going to have to cover for her. Or teach her what she's doing wrong. Or whatever it takes to keep me from knowing just how badly she's performing. Understood?" When they'd all agreed, Eric broached another topic he'd forgotten to mention in the meeting. "And enough of this matchmaking nonsense. I do not want to walk into an exam room and find another single woman without a pet. Do you understand? No pets, no service. Got it?"

"So no more prospective PMWs," Dee said. "Got it."

"And be sure Amy knows."

Again they nodded, though Nancy had the audacity to giggle. Eric gave her his most stern look, which only resulted in causing the other three to join her in chuckles.

"All right. It's funny. Actually," he said sharply, "it's not. I've explained to the girls exactly how I feel about all of this nonsense, and they took it just fine."

After they'd pleaded, argued and just plain got mad at him for being so stubborn about refusing to consider dating anyone, much less some woman who might consider him as a potential mate because she read about him in the paper. But those were details he'd share with no one, not even his mother.

"And another thing," he added. "No more reporters."

"But, Dr. Wilson," Nancy said, "what about that producer from the morning show. Which one was it, Dee? Was it *Today* or *Good Morning America?* I always get them mixed up."

The receptionist frowned. "I've got it in my memo book, but I think it was—"

"No," Eric said before the conversation could continue.

"Oh, come on," his receptionist said. "Are you seriously not excited about the prospect of being on—"

"No" was his final word before he sought the solace of his office and the lunch he had yet to taste.

By the time Amy returned from her lunch break, all remnants of her chaos had been set to rights. Dee went to unlock the door as Amy slid past.

"Uneventful meeting?" she asked.

"Pretty much" was his casual response. "Next week we'll include you," he added as he reached for the topmost charts in the stack. "If you're here, that is."

He waited a moment for her to answer his

implied question. When she offered no further comment other than a nod and a weak smile, Eric returned to his office and busied himself with the ever-growing mountain of paperwork until Dee announced his first client of the afternoon was ready to see him.

"I'm sorry," she added, "but if it helps I've sent Amy in to assist."

"FMW?" Eric asked with a shake of his head.

"That's PMW," Dee corrected. "And I'm afraid we have a few of those scheduled for this afternoon."

To order Dee to call them all and cancel their appointments was tempting, but what if she was wrong and the women were actual clients? "All right," he said as he snapped off the intercom.

Trudging down the hall, Eric paused to lift the slim folder from the holder by the door to exam room one. From the intake folder, it appeared Miss Heidi Varner's Maltese puppy was in need of a checkup. That she came all the way from Galveston to his clinic was a huge red flag, as was the fact the Maltese did not as yet have a name. From the muted sound of female conversation, Amy was already in the room with the client and his owner.

Eric pushed open the door only to find a blonde, tanned and possibly a few years older than expected Miss Varner speaking to another woman via smartphone. Her perfume stopped him short, as did the glittered and glammed-up neon-green dog carrier. Or was it her purse?

"Oh, here he is. Look," she said as she turned to face Eric, lifting her phone so that the caller's face was visible.

Apparently so was his, for the caller, also a peroxide blonde of suspicious age, grinned as broadly as her obviously enhanced lips could manage. "Hey, Doc," she said.

"Um, hello." He looked around the exam room then out into the hall through the open door. Where *was* Amy?

"So I guess you're wondering where my dog is." She gestured to the phone and Eric couldn't help but notice her nails and the shade of neon-pink Miss Varner had applied to them. "Show him, Sara."

The woman disappeared from the phone's screen only to reappear a moment later. She shoved a Maltese puppy up to the lens, and it promptly sniffed heartily then licked the glass.

"Stop it, Fluffer," Sara said before moving the screen a bit farther away from the now-wiggling dog.

Both women looked at him with expectant expressions. "So," he said as he cleared his throat, "how can I help you?"

The instant the words were out, Eric longed to reel them in. Instead, he added, "That is, I'm a little confused why you didn't bring your Maltese in, Miss Varner."

She appeared to be at a loss for a response. Her friend, however, quickly chimed in. "She's thinking of getting one."

Eric resisted the urge to roll his eyes. "Under the circumstances, I think it would be a good idea to get the dog first." He snapped the file shut and turned toward the door. "There will be no charge for today."

"Wait." Miss Varner moved to place herself between Eric and the door, her expression now contrite. "Look," she said as she ended the call and slid the phone into her gaudy green purse. "I really am thinking of getting a Maltese puppy like Sara's." She inched slightly closer and reached to touch his sleeve. "I value your opinion, Dr. Wilson. Or may I call you Eric?"

"Maltese are good dogs," he said. "A little high-strung but if you buy from a reputable seller and check out the lineage thoroughly—"

"I wonder if you might want to meet me after work today." She lifted one painted-on brow. "To check out lineage," she added in what Eric assumed must have been her attempt at a sultry tone. "See, I read about you in the *Houston Chronicle* and I just know we're going to get along fine. I love puppies." She paused. "And little girls."

An image of his three sweet daughters wearing hot-pink nail polish and carrying garish green purses screeched across his mind. Only a shake of his head could dislodge the vision.

"Dr. Wilson, Dee just told me that—" Amy appeared in the door then stopped short, her gaze flitting from him to Miss Varner then back to him. "Oh, I'm sorry. I thought you needed my help." She stifled a smile. "But I can see you're doing fine here so I'll just—"

"Amy, wait." Eric wrestled his sleeve back

from the blonde. "Would you see that Miss Varner gets some literature on what to look for in buying a puppy?"

He backed out of the woman's reach and watched as Amy easily escorted Miss Varner down the hall and out into the reception area. When the coast was clear, Eric escaped to his office and buzzed Dee.

"No more VMWs."

"You mean PMWs?" she asked innocently.

"Whatever you call them, I will not see them." He paused to take a long breath. "Seriously, Dee. If there's even the hint of a possibility that a woman is here to see me instead of have me see her pet, I want you to send Nancy in instead. Do you understand?"

"Yes," she said with what sounded like the beginning of a giggle. "If it makes you feel any better, your next three patients are owned by men. And the one after that's a friend of your mother's."

He scrubbed at his face then closed his eyes. "Just be sure I don't get any more of…those women."

"Yes, sir," she said, this time not bothering to hide her laughter.

A parade of appointments later, all of them with people who owned actual pets, Eric looked up at the clock behind Dee's desk and found it was almost five o'clock. The waiting room was thankfully empty, and the last owner of the day was checking out while chatting with Dee about a sale down at the Grocery Giant. As he stepped behind the counter to deposit the last chart of the day into the filing basket, he noted that somehow a miracle seemed to have taken place.

The office that had been a certifiable disaster since last Friday was neat and orderly. The wastebaskets had been emptied and both of the desks were cleared of all but the in-box and out-box, and even those were no longer overflowing.

Cassie Jo breezed through, purse and tote bag slung over her shoulder. "Done, cleaned up and heading home. See you tomorrow, boss," she said as she disappeared out the back exit.

He barely had a response out before Nancy stepped out of her office and regarded him with a smile. A moment later, Dee walked the client to the front door and let her out then turned the lock.

"So, Dr. Wilson," Dee said, "how was your afternoon?"

"It was fine. Once we sorted out who the real clients were." Eric cast another sweeping glance around the space then shook his head. "Apparently not as good as yours. You certainly got plenty done."

"With Amy's help," Nancy said. "We figured out she doesn't multitask well but if you give her one job at a time, she's great. Really great. She even fixed a paper jam on the printer this afternoon."

"A jam that wasn't her fault," Dee added.

Eric's eyes narrowed. "Where *is* Amy?"

"Your office," Nancy said. "With your girls."

He shook his head. "My girls? Why?"

"Your mom dropped by to see if we could keep an eye on the girls for a few minutes while she ran an errand. I didn't think you'd mind," Nancy said as she gathered up her purse. "You don't, right?"

"No," Eric said though he wasn't sure he believed it. He wanted to trust Amy, but the last time she'd spent time with his daughters he had ended up looking the fool on the front page of the newspaper.

"Need anything else?" Dee asked.

"No, see you both tomorrow," he said over his shoulder as he headed down the hall toward his office.

Eric heard the giggles first and then the soft sound of Amy Spencer growling like a character in the girls' favorite book. He waited only a minute before slowly opening the door.

There he spied Amy sitting on the sofa with Hailey on one side and Ella on the other. Brooke sat in her lap holding the book and turning the pages on cue.

"See, I can read, Amy," Brooke said as she turned the page.

"Cannot," Hailey argued. "You've just heard this story a thousand times and know when to turn the page."

"Do not," Brooke said as she stuck out her tongue.

Ella regarded her sister with a skeptical look that Eric knew all too well. It was the same one he wore far too often. "Do, too," she said. "If you had your way this is the only story we'd hear."

"Is not," Brooke said, her voice rising. "Just because you don't like the story 'cause you're 'fraid of monsters, Hailey."

"Am not," Hailey said.

"Are, too" was Brooke's response.

Eric was about to make his presence known and silence the argument when Amy sprang into action. Resolutely, she closed the book though the story was only half-told.

"Hey," Ella said. "You weren't finished."

"I'm sorry, sweetie," Amy said. "But I only read when there's someone to listen. Otherwise what's the point?"

She asked the question so gently that the girls had no answer but silence. Eric had to smile. He'd have to remember to try that approach next time the girls squabbled.

"I'm listening," Hailey said. "It's just Brooke was—"

"Was not," Brook countered.

"You don't even know what I was gonna say that you were doing."

"Doesn't matter 'cause I wasn't doing it."

"All right," Amy said. "I think there's a

problem here that has nothing to do with reading a book." She paused. "Can one of you tell me what it is?"

Eric leaned against the door frame and listened as the girls took turns guessing what Amy meant. Finally Ella said, "I think we forgot Jesus is listening."

He could see the surprise on Amy's face. "Well, now, that's not exactly what I had in mind, but I would really like for you to tell me more, Ella. What do you mean?"

Ella brightened even as Eric's heart thudded against his chest. He knew what his daughter was about to say.

"That's what our mommy always told us. She said that Jesus always hears us so we should remember to only say what's nice and true."

"And we should treat each other like we want to be treated," Hailey added.

"That's called the Golden Rule," Amy said. "And it's a good rule. You must have had a really smart mommy."

Something in him snapped at the reminder of Christy. Eric threw open the door and held on tight to the frame. "That's quite enough, Amy," he said far too roughly. "You can leave now."

"But she's not finished reading the book, Daddy," Brooke whined as she took the book and climbed off Amy's lap.

"And I was telling her about the Golden Rule," Hailey added.

"And Mama" was Ella's contribution.

Meanwhile Amy rose. Color had risen in her cheeks, a sure sign she was not feeling as calm as she let on. "I bet your daddy can finish reading your book later," she said. "Come back and see me again, okay?"

"Don't count on it." He met her stare. "You said you were leaving Vine Beach soon, remember?"

She opened her mouth to speak then must have thought better of it. Instead, she dipped her head and pressed past him. A moment later, the back door opened then closed again.

"All right, let's get your things and go find Grammy," he said to the girls who were staring at him as if he'd grown a second nose.

"Why were you mean to Amy, Daddy?" Brooke said.

"We like her," Ella added.

"A lot," Hailey said. "And you weren't nice. Remember, Jesus hears everything."

*Apparently not my prayers,* Eric wanted to say. For if they had been heard…

"Everyone to the truck," he said as brightly as he could. "I'll call Grammy and let her know I'm bringing you home. And maybe we'll stop for pizza on the way. Would you like that?"

All three girls let out whoops of joy and went racing down the hall. Eric followed, shutting off the lights and finally locking the back door. While the girls piled into the truck and got situated, he dialed his mother's cell phone.

"I'm sorry, darling. I thought you'd be working late again. I can come right over and get the girls."

"No, it's fine," he told her. "I've got it handled. We're stopping for pizza on the way home."

"Oh, really?"

"Yes, really. Would you like to meet us? The usual place, I'm afraid."

Mom laughed. "Sweetheart, all that noise

and those silly games don't bother me. The girls love it and that's just fine."

The Pizza Palace was a kid's dream and a tired, cranky father's nightmare. Blinking lights on castlelike frescoes competed with a jousting area where children could have a go at one another with what appeared to be horse-shaped pillows. Given the mood his daughters were in, he steered them away from that game and into a nice booth within view of the games but just far enough away to reduce the decibel level to a low roar.

"Can't we play a game before we eat?" Hailey asked as she slid across the semicircular bench and made room for Ella.

Eric helped Brooke get settled then reached for one of the packets of crayons piled in the center of the table and handed it to her. "You know the rule, Hales," he said. "No games until after you eat." He gestured to the menu, a coloring-book-fan's delight. "Look, they've got new ones this week. And it's a princess."

"Look, Ella," she said. "We can color her dress any way we want." She made a grab for a crayon packet.

Soon all three girls were coloring in silence.

If only the volume level on the restaurant's sound track could be muted, as well. Ten minutes later his mother slid into the booth beside Brooke and ordered a diet soda. By then Eric's ears had almost adjusted to the symphony of sounds.

"So, girls," she said, "did Amy take good care of you while Grammy was at the grocery store?"

Ella nodded. "She did until Daddy got mad at her."

"I didn't get mad." Eric turned to his mother. "I didn't."

"Did, too, Daddy," Brooke said. "You told Amy she couldn't read to us anymore."

His mother's eyes widened. "Is this true, Eric?"

He glanced around the table and saw three sets of eyes, all as blue as Christy's, staring up at him. Slowly he let out a long breath. "All right, I might have been a little abrupt with her, but I don't remember saying that."

"You need to tell her you're sorry, Daddy," Brooke said.

Eric nodded. The battle was with him and not with Amy Spencer. "I will, Brookie," he said as he motioned for a waiter. "Next time I see her."

"Promise?" Hailey asked.

He gave his daughter's ponytail a playful tug. "Promise. Now, are you ready to order?" he asked as he turned his attention to his mother.

She hesitated a moment. "Actually, not quite. Do you mind if I speak to you privately, Eric?"

He groaned but agreed, and a moment later they'd walked just far enough away from the table to be out of the girls' ability to hear but close enough to keep watch over them. "All right, Mother, what is it?"

"This thing with Amy," she said as she rested her hand on his arm. "What happened?"

Eric sighed. "Must we talk about this?"

"We must." She tightened her grasp on his arm. "Apparently whatever happened, you've upset the girls over it."

"All right," he said on a long exhale of breath. "It was a busy afternoon. I'd just finished with the last patient. Nancy told me the girls were in my office. That you'd gone to run an errand."

"I hope that was all right," she said.

"Yes, of course." He paused. "I went back to my office and caught Amy reading the girls a story."

She gave him a look. "That seems harmless enough."

He glanced over at the girls then back at his mother. "Maybe. I don't know. But I stopped to listen. Things were fine. And then one of the girls mentioned Christy and something she always said and…"

"And you overreacted," his mother supplied.

"No. Yes." Eric ran his hand through his hair. "Maybe," he finally conceded. "I just didn't expect… That is, hearing her name made me…"

"Miss her terribly?"

He gave his mother a look. "Do you always have to finish my sentences, Mother?"

"I do when you can't" was her swift response. "Or won't."

The two older girls were watching them intently. Brooke, however, continued to color her princess picture oblivious to anything else.

"You know, Eric," she said tentatively, "there's a group for widowed men at church called Starting Over. They have a wonderful group that Riley Burkett leads. Do you know the Holt boy? I think he graduated with you. Jeremy Holt is his name."

He knew Jeremy well. However, he also knew better than to admit anything about the group at this point.

"His mother says he's really enjoying it. You know they play basketball at the meetings. Not sure how that helps a man bounce back into life again." She began to chuckle. "Oh, bounce back. Like a basketball. Now that is clever. I bet Riley thought of that."

"Mother."

"Listen to me, son," she said. "They meet on Saturday mornings. Will you consider going?"

"Yes, I will consider it." He let out a sigh. "Have been considering it, actually."

"Just go once. That's all I ask." She lifted her hand to silence his protest. "Go this Saturday morning. I'll take the girls for another outing and you can go and see what it's like. Will you do that?"

"You know I'm not much of a joiner, Mom." When she gave him a cross look, he continued. "Just once?" he said. "And then no further talk of it?"

"Yes, once is all I ask. Just give it a try."

"All right. Just once." Eric glanced back at the girls, who appeared to be getting rowdy. "Now, what do you say to a pizza and some salad? Looks like my daughters have about reached their tolerance level for being patient."

Her brows rose. "Can I take a quick powder-room trip first?"

Before he could respond, his mother was headed toward the castle doors marked Princesses. "All right, then," he said to her retreating back.

# Chapter Six

The phone rang just as Amy was kicking off her shoes. She glanced at the caller ID and debated whether to answer. *Unknown.* After the conversation with Eric—more of a confrontation, really—the last thing she wanted to do was speak to anyone.

Then again, it could be a potential employer. Thus far she'd heard back from only three of the dozen-plus inquiries, all of them turning her down. Maybe this was the job offer she'd been waiting for. Or at least the interview.

Curiosity got the better of her, and Amy picked up just before the call went to voice mail.

"Amy, dear. This is Susan Wilson. The girls

and I were just about to order pizzas at the Pizza Palace and your name came up." Susan paused as what sounded like circus music rose in the background. "Sorry, but it's a bit loud here. Anyway, won't you come on over? Won't take you five minutes to get here from your grandmother's place and as long as you like pepperoni with extra cheese and a big salad you won't need to look at the menu."

"I'm not so sure your son would want me to—"

"Nonsense," Susan interrupted. "He told me all about the ridiculous way he behaved. He assured the girls and me that he intended to apologize to you the next time he sees you." She paused. "He's not a bad fellow."

"No, of course not." She shifted positions. "But all the same, I—"

"Amy, you would be doing this grandmother a huge favor if you'd come down here. The girls are worried about you. They've all three commented on how, well, they'd be very glad to see you if you'd just join us."

Amy bit her lip and contemplated her options. Pickings in the pantry were slim, and in her haste to leave work, she'd forgotten all about walking down to the grocery store to pick up something for dinner. And while salad fixings grew in abundance in the garden, she really wanted something more substantial.

*What would it hurt?* "All right," she said slowly. "If you're sure Dr. Wilson won't mind. He did say that he didn't want me to—"

"I assure you Dr. Wilson won't be a problem. Now, shall I order a glass of sweet tea for you?"

"Yes, please," Amy said as she slipped her shoes back on.

As Susan predicted, it took only a few minutes for Amy to park her car and find the front door of the Pizza Palace. Between the dizzying array of blinking lights and clanging noises, she might have never found the girls had Ella not bolted toward her to wrap her arms around Amy's middle.

"I'm so glad you're here," she said, her words partly muffled by the volume of the game room nearby. "Come on. I'll show you where we're sitting."

"All right." Amy allowed herself to be led by the eldest Wilson girl. As she turned the corner, she spied the rest of the Wilson family. Including Eric.

She froze as her heart thudded in her chest. What was *he* doing here? Apparently he had the same thought about her as their gazes collided and the color went out of his face. Slowly, he slid to the edge of the bench and rose, releasing Brooke from the confines of her spot in the middle.

"Amy!" Brooke called and ran toward her, arms outstretched.

"Amy, darling!" Susan Wilson rose and moved toward her through the swirl of lights and sounds. "Come join us."

"You didn't mention that your son would be here," she whispered as Susan hugged her.

"Didn't I?" Her face was the mask of innocence, and Amy could almost convince herself of the truth in Susan Wilson's statement. Almost, but not quite.

"Here, sit by me," Hailey said as she yanked at Amy's arm.

"No, me," Brooke said, making a reach across the table for the other hand.

"Don't sit by them," Ella said as she joined the fray. "Sit by me."

"That is quite enough, girls. While you're behaving like that, Amy will sit by none of you." Susan pointed to the empty spot between Eric and the end of the bench. "Go ahead, dear," she said as she pressed her palm against Amy's back.

Before she could claim her seat, Eric reached to grasp her hand. "Amy," he said firmly, "might I have a word with you?"

"He wants to tell you he's sorry," Brooke said.

"Brookie, Daddy can speak for himself," Susan warned. "Go on and sit down, girls." She touched Eric's shoulder. "Perhaps you could speak to Amy later. It appears our pizzas have arrived."

Only when Susan moved away to herd the girls back into the booth did Amy realize Eric still held her hand. She jerked her fingers back and hauled her shaking self into the booth beside Susan. To her horror, Susan scooted the girls around until there was more than ample place for not just Amy but also Eric.

He slid into the only remaining spot, leaving enough room between them so as not to allow his elbow to jostle Amy. This she gave thanks for even as she wondered what in the world Susan Wilson was up to.

Apparently he appreciated his mother's scheming even less than Amy did, for his scowl was instant. "Mother, you know it would have been nice to know—"

"Dear, would you say grace so we can dive in?" she interrupted.

The request appeared to take much of the bluster from the irritated veterinarian, for he lifted his head after the prayer with a much-improved expression. Then came the feast, with three different pizzas—including the promised pepperoni with extra cheese—and a salad of oversize proportions. Amy could only sit back and watch as the girls filled their plates, chattering with exuberance.

So this was what it was like to have sisters. To be part of a family whose easy camaraderie included pizza parties and laughter. As the lone child of older parents, this world was foreign, strange and lovely.

A nudge to her right reminded her that Eric Wilson still sat beside her. She gave him a sideways glance and found him staring.

"You should probably grab a piece before

it's all gone," he told her. "The girls are little but they can put away the pizza."

"Look, Dr. Wilson," she said as quietly as she could, "when your mother called to invite me for pizza with her and the girls, I had no idea you would be here."

His mouth turned up in the beginnings of a smile. "I suspected as much."

"And from your expression, I assume I was a surprise to you, as well."

"Daddy, what are you whispering about?" Brooke said from across the table. "Are you telling Amy you're sorry? 'Cause you said you were going to tell her you were sorry."

"Just some grown-up talk, sweetheart," Eric quickly responded. "Hailey, could you get your sister some salad to go with those three slices of pizza she's got on her plate?" He returned his attention to Amy. "I am sorry, Amy," he said. "I was rude, and I overreacted. Will you forgive me?"

"Of course. I understand." She frowned and swiveled to get a better look at Eric. "That's not true. I don't understand. I can't imagine what it must be like for you, and I'm really sorry."

Her candor must have taken Eric by surprise, for he seemed to be speechless for a moment. Thankfully a waiter appeared with a pitcher of tea, preventing any further discussion on the topic. By the time the waiter had gone, the vet was in a deep discussion with his youngest daughter regarding the best crayon to use on a princess tiara, and Amy had been included in a debate over whether this Saturday's girls' morning should involve swimming at the beach or at the pool.

By the time Hailey and Ella had come to an agreement, Brooke's tiara was colored and Susan was helping her decide on the next thing to work on. A few minutes later, the waiter brought the bill. As Amy reached for her purse, Eric shook his head.

"Oh, no, you don't," he said. "From what I've managed to figure, you're an invited guest. And invited guests don't pay." He punctuated the statement with a look that was probably supposed to be firm. Instead, all she could do was giggle.

"All right," she finally managed. "Thank you."

"Oh, don't thank me." He slid the payment

into the folder then handed it back to the waiter. "Thank my mother."

Susan Wilson looked up from helping Brooke color. "What was that, Eric?"

"Nothing, Mother," he said before turning to wink at Amy. "I'm sure she not only heard every word but she's also listening right now."

The girls' grandmother looked up and quirked a brow. "I am not."

Both Amy and Eric burst into laughter. "See what I have to put up with? A houseful of women plus my mother," Eric said.

"Personally I think it sounds divine."

"Divine?" He shook his head. "You can't be serious."

"I am. I grew up with no brothers or sisters."

"Well, you're lucky," Eric said. "I have sisters, two of them. And an older brother. When everyone's around, we have a houseful."

"Daddy, can we go play the games now?" Hailey asked.

"Yeah, Daddy," Ella added, "you said we could play after we ate."

"So I did." He shrugged. "All right, but you know the rules."

They were off, leaving the three adults at

the table. Susan gathered her purse and stifled a yawn. "If you kids don't need me, I'm going to head home. It's been a long day and I've got an early morning ahead."

"No, that's fine, Mom." Eric rose to give his mother a hug.

"I'll be there at seven-thirty," she said. "That should give all of us plenty of time to get where we need to be."

"Yes, Mother. Now go on and get some sleep. And thank you for keeping the girls occupied today."

She gave Eric another hug then reached to grasp Amy's hand. "I'm very glad you joined us tonight."

"Thank you for the invitation," Amy said. "I had a good time." And she had.

Eric's mother smiled then made her way over to the game room. Once she'd said her goodbyes, Susan waved toward the table then slung her purse over her shoulder and hurried out.

"Well, this is awkward," Eric said as he leaned back and crossed his arms over his chest. "It appears my mother has thrown us together. I'm pretty much oblivious to the ways of women, despite the fact I've got three daughters."

Amy nodded as she took in his statement. Did he regret that she'd joined them or was he just apologizing for the lack of communication on his mother's part?

"Anyway, the girls really like you." He paused. "And I hope you believe me when I say how very sorry I am that I behaved so badly earlier."

"Yes," she said as she studied her napkin rather than the man seated beside her. "Of course."

A familiar squeal went up in the game area, and Amy looked past the vet to see that both Brooke and Hailey wanted to play the same game. Neither appeared ready to compromise.

Eric shrugged. "Sounds like I'm needed. Be right back."

Amy watched him walk away, allowing her mind to wander back to the first time she met Eric Wilson. He'd surprised her while she was sitting in the park reading her book. His presence then had caused her to drop her novel and to ruin her favorite shirt by smearing it with mud. And yet the more lasting impression had been made tonight when she watched him interact with his girls.

She gave passing thought to what his late wife must have been like. With three fair-haired girls, she was probably blonde. What was her name? She tried to recall the conversation where Nancy and Dee spoke in hushed tones about the woman whose death the veterinarian apparently still mourned.

Kristin? No, Christy.

Again she returned her attention to Eric. His dark hair and coffee-colored eyes made him a complete opposite of his daughters. The odd question occurred: Did it bother him that looking at his girls was like looking at his late wife? Of course, this was all conjecture. And Nana always said Amy had an active imagination.

Eric turned to shrug at Amy, presumably over something one of the girls had said. When he returned, he had all three daughters in tow.

"Time to take the girls home," he said. "They've got a big day ahead tomorrow."

"We're going to the beach with Grammy," Brooke said. "And Daddy doesn't get to go."

Amy smiled. "I'm sure Daddy will manage."

"You know, Daddy," Ella said as she slipped her hand into his, "you could always invite Amy to do something tomorrow morning." She glanced up at Amy, her face the mask of innocence. "Are you busy tomorrow morning, Amy?"

"Actually," Eric said quickly, "I have something planned. I'm going to play basketball with some guys up at the church." He met Amy's nervous stare and mouthed a silent "Sorry" before turning his attention back to the girls. "And before you get any bright ideas, Amy cannot go. It's a guys-only thing."

"Hey, now," Hailey said. "What do you mean 'guys-only'? Can't girls play basketball?"

"Probably," Eric said with a grin. "Just not with us."

While Amy appeared to be offended, the girls began to giggle. "You're funny, Daddy," Brooke said. "We're going on a girls-only morning and you're going on a boys-only morning." She gave Amy a stricken look. "But what will Amy do?"

"You could go with us," Hailey said, her expression hopeful.

"Grammy would let you," Ella added. "And we'd like it very much."

Brooke tugged on her sleeve. "We're going swimming at the beach and then we're going to eat somewhere and then we're going to get our toes painted. Do you like getting your toes painted, Amy?"

"I do, but—"

"Then you have to go with us," Hailey said.

"Yes, you just have to." This from Ella.

"Oh, thank you, girls," Amy said. "But I'm afraid I've got plans for tomorrow morning, too."

Brooke stuck out her lip in a look of disappointment. "What are you doing?"

"I have a date," Amy said.

"With who?" Ella demanded.

Amy laughed and ruffled Ella's hair. "My grandmother. I'm going to bring her a picnic breakfast and a porch salad for later, then we're going to look at pictures of her garden. Doesn't that sound like fun?"

Hailey's brows rose. "What's a porch salad?"

"That's where you pick good things to eat

from the garden and, after washing them really well, you chop all the vegetables into a salad and eat it on the porch." She smiled. "Have you ever had a porch salad?"

"No," they all said.

"Well, then," Amy said. "Someday you should try it. It's really good."

She glanced over at Eric and caught him watching her. As their eyes met, he offered her a smile that strangely made her knees weak. Unsettled, Amy looked away.

While the girls gathered their things from the table, Eric leaned over and again apologized. "I just don't understand why they keep wanting to play matchmaker."

"Maybe they love you and want you to be happy." She peered up into his eyes then looked away. "I'm sure they mean well."

"Oh, they do. I'm just not sure how to convince them that when I'm ready, I can manage by myself." His chuckle held little humor. "I somehow managed to catch a wife the first time around."

"How will you know?" The question was out before Amy realized she'd spoken the words. "What I mean is, I struggle with this.

Everything feels so temporary. As if I'm waiting on God to tell me what to do next." She shook her head. "How do you figure out when to do something important like that?"

His gaze collided with hers. "Like leave Vine Beach?"

She nodded.

Eric leaned toward her. "Stay."

"Stay? Simple as that?"

He chuckled. "Simple as that."

Amy was left without a response. At least nothing she could articulate. Her knees, however, had gone weak again and her palms had begun to sweat. And for a moment she could imagine forgetting the fact that her stay in Vine Beach was only temporary.

That she hadn't sent out fifteen inquiries to fifteen employers and only heard back from three.

Thankfully, the girls' laughter filled in the silence that gaped between them. Somehow the trio managed to convince Eric to join them in the game room, leaving Amy the opportunity to plead exhaustion and go home.

The drive was blessedly short, moonlight casting everything it touched in silver. Ocean waves competed with the memory of little-girl giggles to propel her across the lawn and inside the slightly crooked wooden gate.

By porch light, she fitted the key into the lock then opened the door despite its fussy hinges. When Amy stepped inside the empty cottage, a profound sense of emptiness met her. Not just the void where Nana's presence had been, but also the yawning chasm of waiting that seemed to stretch on forever. Then there was the single word that Eric Wilson had uttered: *stay.*

"Too much to think about now," she whispered as she turned off the parlor lamps and walked through to the kitchen.

## Chapter Seven

Eric pulled his truck into the church lot and easily spied the Starting Over group. A dozen men, more or less, were milling around. Several more were shooting baskets, laughter more prevalent than cheers on the court.

He got out and palmed his keys, still unsure whether he would stay. He'd promised his mother to go to the meeting, but he hadn't promised he'd linger.

"That you, Wilson?"

Turning toward the sound, Eric spied Jeremy Holt heading his way. "Hey!"

"Heard you were back in Vine Beach," he said as he jogged up to offer his hand.

"Hey, buddy," he said as he shook hands.

"Only been back a few weeks. What're you doing here?" Eric cringed as he realized how his question sounded. "What I mean is, what do you do here in Vine Beach?"

"I fly for Union Airlines. I'm based out of Houston but with my flight schedule I can live anywhere. Laurie and I wanted to bring up our kids here, so we bought a house and…" He shrugged.

Though his surfer-boy good looks were far behind him, his old teammate on the Vine Beach football team still bore the tanned complexion and fair hair that had earned him a reputation with the ladies back in high school. He knew only a little of Jeremy's story, but what his mother had told him was sad enough. Two years ago Laurie had been killed in an as-yet-unsolved hit-and-run collision.

"And as to the reason I'm here at Starting Over," Jeremy continued, "I've been coming to the meetings awhile. It…" Jeremy looked past the parking lot to the beach. "Well, it helps."

"Yeah, I suppose. I'm just not much of a joiner." He shrugged and turned toward the basketball court. "But I made a promise to my mom that I'd try it just once so I guess I better get to it."

Jeremy laughed and slapped Eric on the back. "How do you think I ended up coming here?" He paused. "Hey, I read that article in the *Gazette.* I'm sorry to hear about Christy."

At the sound of her name, Eric's heart lurched. And yet, it wasn't awful. More like a jab to the ribs rather than a sucker punch to the gut.

"Yeah, I didn't expect the article," Eric said. "More I hear about how that whole thing came about, the more I realize my mother was at the origin of it all."

"I'm sure she means well," Jeremy said. "At first mine tried to fix me up with every single woman she knew between the ages of twenty-five and fifty. And some of the ladies were nice. But I just wasn't ready." Jeremy gestured to the basketball court where the playing had stopped and men were gathering at the far end. "Enough of that. We better step it up or we'll be late."

"Right." Eric followed Jeremy to the court then hung back while his friend stepped through the crowd to speak to an older fellow. A moment later, both men walked toward Eric.

"Welcome," Riley said as he offered up a firm handshake. "Riley Burkett. Glad you're here. Now come on with me and let's get this started."

Eric followed Riley and Jeremy to the center of the court. After a moment of prayer and a short talk on loneliness, Riley broke the men off into groups. "Jeremy, how about you and Eric come with me and we'll chat until it's our turn to play?"

"Play?" Eric shook his head. "So we actually play basketball? I thought it was just something to do until the meeting started."

Riley chuckled. "Well, it's not required. I just figured you'd want to."

"Maybe next time," Jeremy said. "My knee's still giving me trouble." He waved in the direction of the court. "You two go ahead without me. I'm sure you can pick up a third player."

"Actually, I don't mind sitting this round out, either," Eric said.

"All right. What say we find a place in the shade to sit down and talk about today's topic?" When they'd settled on a spot, Riley turned to Eric. "So, you're new, Eric. I don't expect you to participate if you don't want to."

"No, I don't mind." Not that he'd have anything to contribute to this topic. With three daughters and a mother in his private life and a newly busy vet practice, he hadn't had time to be lonely.

"All right. I know you don't have the handout from last week, Eric, so here."

He handed Eric a sheet of yellow paper with a list of questions and spaces left to answer them. The first one made Eric laugh out loud.

Jeremy gave him a look. "What's so funny?"

"Psalm 68:6," Eric said. "The Lord sets the lonely in families? Isn't that the truth. I can't imagine being lonely with the three girls I've got."

"Can't you?" This from Jeremy, who gave Eric a sideways look. "Some of the loneliest times I can remember have been right in the middle of a whole bunch of people who love me."

When Eric didn't respond, Riley nodded. "Might need to think some more about that one, Eric," he said. "Maybe you're fine and don't need a lesson on this topic. It happens like that sometimes." He paused. "Say, didn't

I read in that article about you that you were thinking about putting your boat up for sale?"

Grateful for the change of topic, Eric nodded. "Yeah, actually, I'm still just thinking about it."

"Well, if you were to decide to sell, I'd be interested," Riley said.

"Would you?"

He glanced over toward the marina a few blocks away. "I would. Been wanting to trade up from the little rowboat I've got. Figure I'd best do that before I'm too old to enjoy myself."

An idea dawned. "Hey, since none of us are playing basketball, maybe I could show you the boat. Take her out for a sail?"

The men quickly agreed, piling into Eric's truck to make the short ride to the marina. "There she is," Eric said as he parked and turned off the engine. "That one on the end. With the red-and-white sails."

Riley let out a slow whistle while Jeremy grinned. "Nice," he said as he headed toward the craft.

"Until I moved here, she was purely freshwater. Had her up on Lake Ray Hubbard.

She's good in smooth water, but I have to tell you, I really enjoy taking her out when there's a little chop. Of the two, I prefer the Gulf to the lake. Didn't think I would but she handles so well."

"What's her name?" Riley asked.

"Doesn't have one." Not anymore, he should have added. Not since Christy...

"Might ought to remedy that," Riley responded as he slapped Eric on the back.

"Me or you?" Eric said.

Riley chuckled then gave him a wink. "That remains to be seen, now doesn't it?"

"I suppose so" was his best answer.

A few minutes later they'd weighed anchor and were moving away from the dock. And away from the topic of loneliness, death and dying. At least, Eric intended to leave those conversations back on shore. If the other two wanted to continue their jawing on the subject, they could grab a life vest and swim for the beach.

The glow on Nana's cheeks matched her Vine Beach Garden Club T-shirt of soft crimson emblazoned with the words *Roses are red.* She paired her favorite top with slim white trousers and sandals in matching red. The final touch, tiny ruby earrings, sparkled at her ears. Even now in her wheelchair, her grandmother could easily be mistaken for a woman of much younger years.

To much fanfare from the assembled residents, Amy rolled Nana out of the dining room and away from the din of laughter and conversation that seemed to swirl about every time she visited. While she appreciated the fact that the assisted-living facility was a place where residents enjoyed themselves and the company of others, today Amy needed to be alone with Nana.

She slowed to make the turn at the garden gate then found a shady spot with a picnic table and a nice view of the Gulf. A few minutes later, Amy had unpacked the breakfast she'd made, including fat red strawberries, and was serving up a generous portion to her grandmother.

"Oh, this is wonderful," Nana said. "Looks like the garden is doing us proud this year."

"It is," Amy agreed. "But so are the weeds. I've been fighting quite a battle to keep them out."

"I would guess so," she said. "What with all the rain we had this spring, I'm sure the ground's supporting anything green. What about the marigolds? Are they coming up around the perimeter? They were also good to keep the pests out."

"Just as pretty as always." She reached for her phone and hit the camera button. "Here, look at these. I took pictures of what the garden looked like this morning." Amy handed the phone to Nana. "See, here's how you can go to the next photo."

"Oh, my goodness," she said when she spied the rose bushes. "They're going to be filled with blooms in another month."

"They are," Amy said. "And they already smell heavenly."

Nana glanced up, her face wistful. "Will you bring me some next time you're here? I'd love to have roses for my apartment. And of course I have to show them off. I might not be president of the rose club anymore but I sure am the record holder for best bloom. Can't even recall how many times I've won."

Amy knew better. Every single trophy and plaque had been carefully packed up and moved to the little apartment in the assisted-living facility. The collection now held a place of honor in a cabinet just inside the front door. And never had she seen even a speck of dust on one of the shiny prizes.

"I'm sorry I didn't think of bringing any," she said. "But I'll be sure you have a big bouquet next time I'm here. And more of the salad like the one I brought you for lunch later."

"Oh, and, sweetheart, could you bring some shells for my nightstand? You know how I love that little reminder of living at the beach."

"I'll bring some from the house," she said.

Nana shook her head. "If you don't mind, could you bring me some fresh?"

"Fresh?" Amy said. "What do you mean?"

"Please don't think I'm a silly old lady, but I would really love to have some shells that had slept on the beach recently. You know... fresh."

Amy joined her grandmother in a smile. "If that's what you want," she said, "then that's what you'll have. Now, what do you think of the pictures?"

"Thank you for bringing them, Amy. The pictures are very nice," she said as she handed the phone back to Amy. "Maybe I need one of those fancy phones. What do you think?"

"I think you'd probably love it." She grinned and Nana did, too.

"Well, be that as it may, I don't know who I'd call," she said. "Most of my friends are either here or down at the cemetery." At Amy's raised brow, Nana chuckled. "Now don't you get all fussy with me. No one lives forever. I'm a realist. Any day I wake up is a good one, but the day I go home to Jesus will be the best of all." She took a bite of the breakfast casserole then set her fork down. "Not that I'm any hurry to go, mind you."

"Yes, ma'am," Amy said.

For a moment the only sound was the crashing waves and the occasional car driving past. A sailboat with red-and-white sails glided by on the horizon, and Amy's gaze followed the craft until it disappeared from view.

"You're awfully quiet," Nana said. "Something bothering you or am I just that boring nowadays?"

"What? Nana, no." Amy shook her head. "You're not boring at all. I was just...thinking."

She peered at Amy over her silver-rimmed glasses. "I see. So," she said slowly, "might you be thinking of Susan's boy?"

"Eric? No." Amy shook her head, partly to rid herself of the thought of those coffee-colored eyes staring at her as he urged her to stay in Vine Beach. "Not specifically," she finally said as she took a bite of a juicy strawberry.

"Then what is it?" Nana reached for her glass of iced tea and held it up to take a sip. "Specifically."

"All right." Amy sat her fork down. "Specifically, I'm confused. I just don't know..." She shook her head. "Nana, we've already talked about this. I'm just confused. I thought my stay here in Vine Beach was only temporary."

"Yes, I recall telling you to do the last thing God told you until He led you to the next one." Nana lifted a pale brow. "So what's the problem?"

"The problem is, I haven't heard from any of the jobs I applied for in Houston or Dallas, so I'm left to assume they're not interested. I just can't figure out what that next thing is."

"Why do you have to figure it out?" She returned her tea glass to the table and reached for another strawberry then pointed it at Amy. "Must you always have the answers to the questions in your time? Just bloom where you're planted, Amy. That's all there is to it."

*Bloom where you're planted.*

The statement followed Amy back to Nana's apartment and then chased her home afterward. If only it were so simple.

But then hadn't she said that to Eric Wilson just last night?

# Chapter Eight

Brilliant midmorning sunshine glinted off the swells and shone a path between the sailboat and the horizon. The chop was slight, the breeze stiff and the sky a cloudless blue. Perfect sailing weather.

As Eric trimmed the sails, he half listened to the spirited conversation going on between Riley and Jeremy. Something about a college football game. And then they grew quiet. Riley placed his hand on Jeremy's shoulder and Jeremy looked away.

A moment later it appeared as if both men had their heads bowed in prayer.

Private business, Eric decided. Probably something to do with the reason Jeremy attended Starting Over. It took another half hour before Riley came up to Eric and sat down beside him.

Eric gestured to the wheel. "Want to try her out?"

Riley's sideways look made Eric grin. "Sure do," the older man said as he took the wheel and guided the craft like an expert.

"You've done this a time or two," Eric said when he took the wheel once again. "Nice sailing, sir."

He leaned back and crossed his legs at the ankles. "Well, she's a nice boat, son. Handles like a dream and easy to look at. You sure you're ready to sell her?"

"No," Eric said. "I'm not so sure anymore. Still want to be the first to know if I change my mind?"

The older man chuckled. "That I do." He paused as his expression sobered. "You know, Eric, you won't lose what you had with your wife. Ever."

The statement, bold as it was, surprised Eric. He looked across the deck at Jeremy, who was absorbed with watching the dolphins dance along in the vessel's wake and did not seem to hear.

"I already have lost what I had with her" was Eric's swift reply when he returned his attention to Riley. "She's not here, Riley. Or hadn't you noticed?"

Riley's smile did not waver, nor apparently did his determination to continue with the topic. "What I noticed is a man whose girls mean the world to him. A family man. What you had with your wife lives on through those girls. In a way, you're blessed to have that."

"I'm blessed to have *them*," Eric corrected, "but as to the rest of it, I'd have to respectfully disagree on the blessing part."

"I can see how you'd think that." He lifted his cap to run his hand through thick gray hair. "I'd like to believe, however, that the Lord brings us blessings for a season." Riley replaced his cap on his head then situated it until it was just right. "Not every man can say he's been well and truly loved. Can you say that?"

Eric opened his mouth to respond but found the words stuck in his throat. Instead, he settled for a nod.

"Then that's a blessing. You can't put a time limit on that."

"I guess not," Eric said without much enthusiasm.

"And I guess if you were given the option of having her for the short time you had her or never getting hurt by never having her, well, you'd choose to let it play out just the way it has."

"Sorry, Riley, but if I could choose, I'd choose to never lose her."

Riley clasped his hand on Eric's shoulder. "Well, of course you would. I would, too." He looked past Eric, presumably to the waves the boat's hull so easily sliced through. "But we don't get to choose, nor do we get to tell the Lord His business. And when He chooses to take each of us is His business."

Eric dipped his head. "I can't argue with that."

The older man patted Eric's shoulder. "Me, either," he said. "Though there are plenty of times that I'd like to."

They sailed the rest of the way in silence. A short time later, the vessel tied at anchor, Eric dropped Jeremy and Riley off at the now-deserted church parking lot with a promise to consider returning next week. He'd made his customary left onto Main Street when he realized he'd left his sunglasses back on the boat.

Making a U-turn at the light, Eric headed back to retrieve them. He found the shades and put them on then headed back to the truck. Windows rolled down, he cranked the engine and shifted into Drive. He'd just turned onto Vine Beach Drive when he looked ahead and saw Amy Spencer crossing the road from the beach to her house with a basket in the crook of her arm.

Her grandmother's house, he corrected.

Amy wore a white tank top over denim shorts, and a tiny cross on a silver chain glittered at her neck. Golden curls tossed in the sea breeze, and she used her free hand in a poor attempt to tame them. He only thought a second before honking the horn. She waved, and he stopped. Eric gestured to the basket. "What do you have there?"

She looked down at the basket then back up at Eric. "Fresh shells."

"Fresh shells? What in the world is that?"

Amy tugged at the hem of her top, allowing the wind to blow a strand of hair across her forehead. "It's kind of a long story," she said as she swiped at the curl.

"Well," he said before he let himself hit the gas and flee, "if you've got time to tell it, I've got time to listen."

Only pausing a second, Amy nodded. "I could use a glass of iced tea and a slice of coconut cake. How about you?"

A nod and she was off. Eric waited until she'd reached the porch steps before easing the truck into the driveway. Unlike last time, Eric paused to take in the Victorian beauty that was the Spencer home. All porches, picket fence and windows, the white-trimmed cottage was neither grand nor imposing. Rather, it held a welcoming charm that seemed to bid a man to come and sit awhile.

By the time he climbed out of the vehicle, Amy had the door unlocked and was depositing her basket of shells on a table just inside.

"Be right out," she said. "Make yourself comfortable."

"All right," he called as he made his way around the waist-high picket fence to the front walk, punctuated by newel posts that were capped in matching white. The concrete walkway split the green lawn in half, with the portion to his right filled with several shade trees and a small birdbath that glistened with fresh water. Circling the birdbath was some sort of flowering plant that butterflies appeared to enjoy. As he stepped inside the yard, a great orange-and-black monarch butterfly darted across his path. From the shadows, a black-and-orange tabby shot out to make a futile attempt at capturing its flying prey. When Eric laughed, the feline shot him a nasty look and slipped beneath a low spot in the fence to disappear.

Out of the corner of his eye, Eric saw the butterfly land again, this time on the newel post to his left. He reached to touch the butterfly and it danced away, following the gravel path that meandered to the left of the center walk then disappeared behind an arbor covered in roses. Something white hung inside the arbor, but from where he stood, Eric couldn't quite make out what it was.

He ascended the stairs and thought once again of the condition of the stair rail. One of Riley's ideas about beating the battle of loneliness was to go out and do something for someone else. A couple of the guys had talked about how they'd volunteered here or there or done handyman projects for folks who couldn't manage things on their own.

Reaching over, he gave the rail a good shake and watched while paint chips fell like snow on the concrete. Maybe this was his project.

Not that he was lonely. No, definitely not.

But it would be good to do something for someone else. Maybe he'd get the girls out to help, too.

Soon as the thought occurred, Eric dismissed it. Knowing what those three did with frosting or finger paints, it would be a very long time before he allowed them free use of anything as permanent as house paint.

Eric stepped up onto the porch and glanced to his left where a pair of white rocking chairs moved slightly in the breeze. Between them was a small wicker table that held a book and a half-burned citronella candle. He walked past the chairs, setting one in motion as he reached for the book. With its smudge of mud, it had to be the novel Amy was reading in the park that day.

Eric picked it up and turned it to read the back. But his thoughts landed on the classifieds girl. She'd looked so pretty that day that he'd almost been compelled to go and say hello. Though it hadn't been for her beauty alone that he'd stopped. There was something else, what he hadn't yet decided.

But whatever it was, it now held him captive on a sun-drenched porch waiting for iced tea and cake.

He took a few more steps and reached the porch rail. Unlike the rail on the stairs, this one seemed sturdy enough and the paint looked good. Just out of reach was the arbor, also white he could now see, that bore the weight of a fragrant climbing rose. Hung under the twisting branches was a white-washed porch swing, its chain rusted and creaking as it moved back and forth.

It wasn't hard to imagine what the view of the beach would be from that swing. And from the sag in the seat, it also wasn't hard to imagine that a generation or two of Spencers had enjoyed the spot. The monarch butterfly dipped beneath the trellis then darted out the other side to disappear around the back of the house.

"I hope you like your tea sweet."

Eric turned around at the sound of Amy's voice. She'd slipped a pink shirt over her tank top but left it unbuttoned, the tails hanging loose, and her bare feet were now encased in pink sandals. In her hands was a tray that held a pitcher of tea, two glasses and a double serving of coconut cake. Nodding toward the table on the other side of the porch, she carried the tray over and set them down.

He followed and watched as Amy poured tea and then settled onto a chair in the shade. The butterfly returned to alight on the porch rail, its wings fluttering in the dappled shade.

"Are you just going to stand there or do I have to eat cake alone?" Amy grinned. "Not that this would be a new thing."

Chuckling, he took the chair across from Amy and accepted the glass she handed him. It was sweet and cold and exactly what he needed. Not that he'd known he needed it until just then.

"You look a little sunburned," she said as she gestured toward his nose. "Been out on the water in that sailboat today?"

"I have, actually." He took one more swallow then set the glass down. "Took a couple of friends out. Might have a buyer for the boat so I won't have to place that ad, after all."

At the reminder of the *Gazette,* Amy's gaze lowered even as she smiled. "Guess it will be a relief to have it sold."

"Not really." Eric leaned back in his chair and watched Amy divide the cake into two slices. "Thanks to a certain reporter and her accomplices, my vet practice is in the black way ahead of schedule. Thus, the need to sell the boat is not as pressing."

This time rather than deflect her gaze, Amy captured his stare and held it. "About that."

Eric waved away any further response. "Nope. No need to talk about it. All water under the bridge, as my mother would say."

"Do you really feel that way, Eric?" She handed him a slice of cake on a plate more suitable to a ladies' tearoom than the front porch of a beach cottage.

"I didn't," he admitted as he picked up a silver fork. "But now I do." He sighed. "Look, Amy, I do. What point is there in holding a grudge?"

"True," she said slowly.

"And I believe that none of you meant to cause any trouble." Eric shook his head. "No, I can't let my mother and daughters off so lightly. I know that *you* didn't intend to. Let's just leave it at that."

Eric jabbed his fork into a bite of the best coconut cake he'd ever tasted, his mother's included. He was about to say so when Amy pointed in his direction.

"And just to remind you, I'm not a reporter. Or rather, I wasn't one. I just answered the phones in the classifieds."

"Duly noted." He set down his fork and held up his glass of tea as if toasting her. "Though with your talent for coconut cakes, you'd do well to consider a career in baking."

"I'll tell Nana you said so." Amy's smile grew. "She may be in the assisted-living community, but no one has to help her with the cooking." She paused as if thinking of something that made her look sad. "I miss her. Miss her here, that is." Meeting his gaze, she shrugged. "But she's happy and that's what counts. And because she has most of her meals with her friends in the facility's dining room, I benefit by taking home the baked goods she can't help herself from making."

"Sounds like a fair trade."

"It is," she agreed. "Though I'm going to have to take up running again if she doesn't stop making this cake. I've been giving most of what she sends me to the nice couple next door. They're not much younger than Nana, but Mr. King comes and cuts my grass for me when I don't get to it first. And Mrs. King supplies me with stories of my dad and her son and their antics growing up together. She's highly entertaining, and apparently so was my father."

"Where's your father now, if you don't mind my asking?"

"Houston. He and Mom own a flower shop in Rice Village. I used to work with them until Nana's hip-replacement surgery." She paused as her fingers worried with the cross at her neck. "It was simpler for me to leave and come down to help Nana than for either of them to do it."

"I see."

Amy shrugged. "I was the one who wouldn't be missed."

He gave her a sideways look then lifted one brow. "I doubt that. I know you've left a lasting impression on me."

She laughed. "Eat your cake, Eric."

A comfortable silence settled around them as Eric enjoyed the cake almost as much as he enjoyed watching Amy. Somehow he'd missed how gracefully she moved. How lovely the light dusting of freckles across her cheeks were. And how very much he liked her laugh.

"Will you miss your sailboat?"

Eric jolted to attention. "Well, I still have it so…" He shook his head. "Yes, very much. It's been a long time since I enjoyed myself like I did today."

"Oh?"

"Christy and I had her docked up at Lake Ray Hubbard, so she's not had much salt water under her." He smiled. "It was great."

"You have a nice smile." Soon as she said it, Amy cringed. "Sorry, that didn't come out right. What I mean is, you should smile more often." She waved away his response. "Never mind. That didn't sound good, either."

"No," Eric said gently. "I know what you

mean. I guess I just haven't had much to smile about for a long time."

"How long?"

He knew what she meant. Knew also that this time she wasn't apologizing for what she'd said. Rather, she just seemed interested. As if she cared.

"Almost four years," he said on an exhale of breath. Before she could ask, he added, "Cancer."

She reached across the distance between them, navigating the plates and tea glasses to place her hand atop his. "I'm sorry."

"Me, too," he said. "It changed everything."

Amy leaned back and pulled her hand away gently as she reached for the tea pitcher to refill his glass. "Things like that do," she said softly.

And then she changed the subject. First to talk about the proliferation of monarch butterflies that had enjoyed her grandmother's early summer garden. Then to the neighbor's cat who hid in the garden and chased out all form of critters, except for the butterflies. They'd moved on to speak of life in Vine Beach, of what Eric remembered growing up as compared to what Amy found when she spent summers here, when Eric stopped to point at her.

"You used to get dragged to those awful Garden Club meetings, too, didn't you?"

She laughed. "I wouldn't say they were awful, but I will confess that I had to be bribed with ice cream not to pitch a fit about going. Why?"

"Because I had to go to them, too." He gave her an appraising look. "You had glasses. Red or maybe…"

"Pink," she supplied.

Eric snapped his fingers then pointed at her. "Yes, pink. And you wore your hair in this braid down your back."

"French braid," she corrected, "and it was quite the ordeal to get it just right. I would spend hours in front of the mirror trying to get it just so. Drove poor Grandpa crazy when I'd monopolize the only bathroom in the house." She shook her head. "But I don't remember you."

He laughed. "That's because I hid. I hated those stupid things but someone had to carry the plants for my mom. Dad and I made a deal. Every time I volunteered to go instead of him, he'd slip me a twenty on my way out the door. Made it worth my while."

"Interesting that I could be bribed with ice cream while it took cash to persuade you."

Eric winked. "You ply me with enough of this coconut cake and I could just about be persuaded to do whatever you ask." Now it was his turn to cringe. "Okay, that didn't come out right. What I mean is…" He shook his head. "Never mind. What I mean is, this is good cake."

"So you said," she responded with a chuckle.

"I seem to remember you always had your nose in a book." He gestured to the table between the rockers. "Guess that hasn't changed."

"Nope. I've usually got a porch book going, a bedside-table book going and sometimes one more just for good measure."

"Really?" He shook his head. "Not sure I know the difference between those."

"Well, a porch book is kind of like a beach read." She waited until he shook his head, indicating he was clueless as to her meaning. "All right, well, it's one that you don't have to think too hard about. Funny, maybe, or at least not deep."

"All right," he said. "And a bedside-table book?"

"Oh, that's one that you take to bed and read. It's anything but scary. I sleep in a room up in the rafters, you see, and this old house creaks. So, nothing scary."

"Got it. What are you reading now?"

She told him, starting with the porch book and then moving on to the bedside-table book. All the while, he sipped tea and feasted on coconut cake. Then he shared with her the suspense novel that the girls made it almost impossible to read. Told her how many times he'd started the book only to put it down, not because he wasn't enthralled with the adventure but because he was more interested in the adventure that was being a single dad.

From there the conversation moved on to the topic of fresh shells. He'd never laughed so hard as when Amy explained the difference that, as it turned out, her grandmother had not only mentioned that morning but had already called to remind her about while she was on the beach looking for them. Apparently grandmothers and children were persistent creatures, a topic they also discussed at length.

It was the best time he'd had in ages.

Then it hit him. The guilt that always lay in wait in the dark corners of his world. That slice to the gut that reminded Eric that he was free to inhale deep breaths of this glorious life and Christy was not.

"I should go." He stumbled up from his chair, the absurd weight of the stupid emotions rendering him unable to be any more graceful that he might have otherwise. "Thank you for the tea and cake."

Somehow he was up and moving, taking the steps two at a time and jarring the rail so hard it leaned to one side. "I'll be back to fix that," he said, though he hoped she wouldn't hold him to it.

Only when the truck's engine cranked to life and the air-conditioning blew in his face did Eric feel as if he could truly breathe again. He rolled up the windows and sat for a moment to let himself and the truck cool off. As he shifted the truck into gear, he spied Amy picking up the remains of their feast, watched her disappear inside and then heard the screen door slam.

Eric's finger jabbed the radio button, and he punched the buttons until he found a song that fit his mood. Then he turned it up. Loud. Just as he would have before…

"No," he said, as he drummed the pounding rhythm with one hand while guiding the truck onto Vine Street with the other.

And though the music was loud enough to cause raised eyebrows in the car that stopped next to him at the light, it still couldn't compete in Eric's mind with the sound of Amy's laughter.

And the slam of the screen door.

# Chapter Nine

$\sim$

Amy placed her lunch in the break-room refrigerator and turned around to see Cassie Jo awaiting her turn. "Sorry," she said as she scooted out of the way to allow the groomer to place her paper sack and soda alongside Amy's.

She glanced at the clock. A quarter to nine. The clinic wouldn't open for another fifteen minutes. Just as well. Amy needed all of those fifteen minutes and more to prepare herself for seeing Eric Wilson again.

All weekend she'd tried to figure out just where their lovely visit went wrong. It was he who stopped her on Vine Street. He who invited himself up for a chat about fresh shells and books and had entertained her with stories about his girls. And he who had abruptly raced off without so much as an explanation.

Every time Amy passed the stair rail, which now listed sadly to the right, she wondered what she'd done wrong. She also hoped she could convince Mr. King to look at it before Eric made good on his promise to fix it.

Thus, yesterday she'd decided to forgo her usual spot in the pew behind the Wilson family to attend the church service at the assisted-living facility. If Nana had seemed suspicious, she didn't indicate it. Instead, she went on about the lovely vase full of shells Amy had carefully arranged and delivered along with a few jars of canned vegetables that Nana had requested. And she'd said nothing about Eric Wilson or his mother.

That had been the biggest blessing of all.

The back door opened and closed, causing the alarm to chirp and bringing Amy back to the present. Cassie Jo breezed past, her ponytail swinging.

At the break-room door, Cassie Jo turned. "Oh, it's not nine yet. That means I've still got a few minutes before my first client." She leaned against the door frame. "So, Amy, how was your weekend?"

Amy was about to respond when Eric appeared in the hall behind the groomer. He seemed to pause just a moment and then he spied her and hurried past. Or at least that was how it appeared.

She managed some sort of passable answer to Cassie Jo then pressed past her to head to her desk. Filing and paperwork kept Amy busy until lunchtime. Apparently something kept Eric busy, as well, for he didn't make a single appearance in the front office all morning.

When the last patient of the morning had been seen and sent out the front door, Dee locked the entrance and indicated it was now officially lunchtime for the staff.

"Be there in just a second," she said as she took the last three files of the morning to the file room. "Just want to finish this up."

"All right," Nancy called, "but you know how finicky the ice maker's been acting. If there's none left when you get there, it's your own fault."

"A chance I'll just have to take," she called as she bent down to the correct file drawer.

A noise behind her caused Amy to straighten. When she turned toward the door, she locked eyes with Eric. He stood as if frozen, a file in his hand and a brilliant shade of red climbing up his neck and into his cheeks.

"I thought everyone was in the break room," he said after clearing his throat twice. "But apparently not."

Business or personal, which direction to go in her response? "Would you like that filed?" she finally asked.

Eric looked down, apparently surprised he still held something. "This? Oh, yes, please. I was given the wrong Miller. This is Brenda. I need Becca."

"Of course. Sorry about that." When he seemed unable to move, Amy moved toward him and took the file from his hand. "Do you want the other one now or should I put it on your desk?"

He recovered sufficiently to shake his head. "Just put it in the basket for my afternoon patients. This one's a callback and I figured I'd do that later."

"All right."

She turned toward the files and, before she

opened the correct drawer, heard footsteps walking away. Odd how he'd been acting so different around her.

A moment later, with the correct Miller file in hand, Amy walked into the empty front office to deposit it in the afternoon basket. A glint of sunlight cut across the window, and she looked over to see Eric's truck leaving the parking lot.

With nothing left to keep her busy, Amy picked up the novel from her desk and walked down the hall to the break room to retrieve her lunch from the fridge. Nancy and Dee were embroiled in a debate about where to order lunch for Wednesday's staff meeting, while Cassie Jo munched on a peanut-butter sandwich looking more than a little amused.

"All right," she said to Amy. "Give it up. What's going on with you and Dr. Wilson?"

The other conversation came to a screeching halt as Dee and Nancy turned to stare. "What's this?" Dee asked while Nancy's brows rose even as her mouth stayed firmly shut.

"I don't know what you're talking about,"

Amy said as she unzipped her lunch container with shaking hands.

"Come on," Cassie Jo said to the others. "Don't tell me you haven't noticed it."

"Noticed what?" Dee asked.

"The tension around here." Cassie Jo grinned. "The question is, why is he running from someone on Monday who made him smile at the pizza parlor on Friday?" She grinned. "And yes, I have my spies. It's all over Vine Beach that you and Dr. Wilson were seen enjoying a cozy dinner with his girls."

"And his mother," Amy said. "Who, by the way, invited me without bothering to mention that her son would be there." When they all stared with disbelieving looks, she added, "It's true. Believe it or not, I may be the only single woman in Vine Beach who does *not* have designs on Eric Wilson."

"Well, that's a relief," a familiar deep voice said from the door.

Amy swung her attention from the surprised trio to see the man in question standing just outside in the hall. Closing her eyes, she groaned.

"Nancy," Eric said. "Where did you put the new credit card? I just tried to fill up the truck and noticed it was expired."

She jumped up and scurried out of the office, ducking past Eric as she looked back into the break room with a horrified expression. Dee ducked her head and concentrated on her chicken-salad sandwich while Cassie Jo stared without concealing her interest.

Finding nothing to say, Amy reached for the book she'd carried in and held it in front of her. Though the words swam on the page and she couldn't recall a thing she read, Amy continued pretending an interest in the novel.

"Beach or bedside?" This from the man who'd avoided her all morning then couldn't be bothered to offer a polite goodbye.

Cassie Jo giggled as Dee turned toward Eric, her surprise evident. "See," Cassie Jo said. "I told you something was—"

"Here it is, Dr. Wilson," Nancy called, and he turned toward her.

"Thank you, Nancy." Eric pulled his wallet out of his back pocket and removed the old card, exchanging it with the one Nancy held. "Be sure to dispose of that one properly."

"Will do, boss." Nancy turned to see the expressions on her coworkers' faces. "What?" she demanded. Then she returned her attention to Eric. "What did I miss?"

The veterinarian had the audacity to shrug. "Beats me. I was just inquiring about reading materials." And then he was gone, once again without warning or benefit of saying goodbye.

No one spoke until the back door closed. And then all three of them began to speak at once. Amy ducked her head and closed her eyes. What to say?

When she lifted her head, the room grew quiet. "So?" Cassie Jo said. "Bedside or beach? What kind of code is that?"

"Probably not the kind you think," she snapped. Amy took a deep breath and let it out slowly as she replaced her bookmark and set the novel aside. "He is referring to a conversation we had once about books. How some are beach books. Porch books, really. Others are for bedside tables. You know, the books you'd read before you fall asleep."

No one spoke. Nor did they appear to believe a word of her explanation.

"Come on," Amy continued. "You know

what I mean. No one wants to read a ghost story before bed, and you sure don't want to be slugging your way through some treatise on economics or politics while sitting on the beach."

"Riiight," Dee said. "You wouldn't want that."

"Noooo," Nancy echoed.

This time Cassie Jo stared without comment, though she did wear an I-told-you-so look.

Amy zipped up her lunch container and gathered her drink then rose to deposit both in the refrigerator. Without saying a word, she squared her shoulders, straightened her spine and walked out of the break room without managing to show the tears that were threatening. Ten minutes later, she left the staff restroom with no evidence that she'd been crying.

At least she hoped that was the case.

When she returned to her desk, Dee had printed out the afternoon file list. She gratefully took it into the file room without meeting Nancy's or Dee's silent questioning stares. Opening the first file, she retrieved the needed documents then shut the drawer. That's when she spied Cassie Jo standing where Eric had been before lunch.

"I'm sorry," she said. "I was only teasing. I didn't mean…" She shrugged and seemed near tears. "Will you forgive me?"

Amy's smile dawned slowly and in spite of the feelings still swirling around her. "Yes, of course. I know you didn't mean anything by it."

"I truly didn't. It's just that, well, I've suspected something ever since I saw the doc trotting across Main Street to chat you up and make you drop that book." She shrugged. "Couldn't help it. We've all been praying he found someone and, well, we thought maybe he had. He came back from the park with a grin on his face that lasted a good while. And that was after telling us just the day before at our staff meeting that the practice was in trouble. He'd been awfully reserved, of course, and for good reason. Well, that and the fact he lost his…" She seemed unwilling to complete the statement.

"His wife?" she supplied. "Yes, I know."

She let out a little giggle then clasped her hand over her mouth. "Oh, goodness, what's wrong with me? Of course you knew, what with that article in the paper and all."

"Right."

"Right," Cassie Jo echoed as she toyed with her ponytail.

Amy waited a minute, then, when it appeared Cassie Jo had nothing else to say, she went back to her work. Just last Friday, Eric had told her to stay.

Now all she could think about was how she could manage to go. Telling Eric she was leaving might do the trick, though she hadn't yet figured out where her destination was. Thus, she decided to do as Nana said and wait until God told her what the next thing was to be.

To bloom where she was planted, even if the other flowers in the Wilson Vet Clinic garden stared at her as if she were the wrong variety and despite the fact the weather surrounding Eric Wilson ranged from hot to cold without much warning.

As if on cue, the man himself returned from lunch. Barely sparing anyone a backward glance, he strode through the front office and snagged the stack of files for the afternoon patients. "Go ahead and open the door, Dee," he called as he headed for the hall then stopped short. "Mr. Carson's been pacing out front with his hunting dogs for the past five minutes so our clocks must be slow. Or at least that's what he just told me in the back parking lot."

"Yes, sir," Dee said as she jumped up and grabbed the keys.

"And, Nancy, see that the lab work is back for the Prines' cat. I need to call Mrs. Prine and let her know whether a prescription's in order."

"Yes, Doctor," she said as she hurried off to check the fax machine.

Cassie Jo slipped out mumbling some excuse about checking the shampoo order before the UPS man came, leaving Amy alone with Eric. He seemed preoccupied reading a file, but Amy suspected he was anything but.

"Bedside," she said firmly, maintaining an even expression when Eric's gaze collided with hers.

"I'm sorry?" He closed the file and held it against his chest. "What did you say?"

Amy swallowed hard and stilled her quaking knees. "You asked me a question about my book earlier, Eric. And the answer is bedside." She paused to swallow the last of her emotions. "Because it's not scary." Another pause. "Thank you for asking."

Before she could say more or, worse, Eric could respond, Amy pressed past him to return to the file room. This time she closed the door behind her. If Eric intended to discuss anything further, at least she'd be forewarned by hearing the door open.

But the door did not open, nor did Eric indicate that he had any interest in speaking to her at all.

# Chapter Ten

"Really, Daddy?" Hailey squealed while her sisters danced around the kitchen making a similar joyful noise. "Really can we really go sailing tomorrow?"

"Really, Eric?" his mother echoed. "Are you sure?"

He gave his mother a look that he hoped would remind her who was in charge of making decisions for the girls. "Yes, Mother, I'm sure." Eric paused to soften both his tone and his expression. "There are life jackets for each of them, and the girls know how to swim." He ruffled Brooke's curls. "Not that I intend any of them to use their skills. Do I, Brookie?"

"No, Daddy. We're to sit still and mind whatever you say while we're on the sailboat." The five-year-old's gap-toothed grin melted his heart.

"That's right." He watched his mother's disapproval fade as the girls' enthusiasm grew. "All right, girls. Thank Grammy for keeping an eye on you today then go and take Skipper out back and run around with him. I'd like him good and tired so he goes to bed early."

A chorus of thank-yous rang out, followed by hugs and kisses, and punctuated by Skipper's exited yips. Finally, after the girls and Skipper had disappeared into the backyard, his mother leaned in to touch his sleeve. "Where did you learn that trick?" she said with a twinkle in her eye.

Eric chuckled. "C'mon, Mom. Do you think at some point we didn't figure out that running around with the dog wasn't to make the dog tired? Bandit seemed to sleep pretty well without our help."

She joined in his laughter then abruptly sobered. "Now, about that sail tomorrow. Have you thought this through? Brooke's just a baby. And the other girls sometimes want to go their own way rather than listen."

"You're really worried about this."

She crossed her arms over her chest. "I am."

Eric considered inviting his mom along to help. Taking her along, however, would defeat the purpose of spending time alone with the girls.

Thus, he gently turned Mom toward the door and linked arms to walk with her. "Thank you for worrying. Really. I promise I won't take any risks with the girls."

She opened her mouth as if to say something then must have thought better of it. Closing her mouth tightly, his mother settled for a squeeze of his hand.

He paused to let her retrieve her purse. When Mom straightened, Eric gave her a hug. "You know I can't lose anyone else I love. I just can't." At his mother's nod, he continued. "We'll take the boat out to Sandy Island. Bring a picnic. I think the girls will like that. That's close to shore but far enough out to make them feel like they've been on a real cruise." He paused. "I promise they'll be well supervised. What do you think of that?"

She clutched her purse and slowly a smile dawned. "I think that sounds wonderful. But will you do one thing for me?"

"What's that?" he asked as he prayed she was not making an attempt to invite herself along. "Within reason," Eric added.

"Will you call me when you get the girls back on dry land?" She looked down to study her nails then back up at Eric. "You're not the only one who can't lose another person they love."

Eric enveloped his mother in an embrace and felt for the first time how tiny she'd become since his father's death. "Of course I will, Mom," he whispered against her ear. "And we'll take pictures, too. How's that?"

Mom slipped out of his embrace and pointed her finger at him. "You'd better." She grinned. "And don't let Brookie use the camera. Last time I let her near water with mine she dropped it in."

"Oh, no, Mom. I'm sorry. Why didn't you tell me?"

She lifted a silver brow. "Don't be silly, darling. It was an accident, and it was time for a new camera, anyway."

"Daddy!" Ella shouted from the backyard. "Brooke's turned on the water hose and Skipper's all wet!"

"So are we," Hailey called as Skipper began to bark.

"Time to go supervise," Eric said as he gave his mother one last hug and sent her on her way. "See you tomorrow, Mom."

He walked into the backyard to find a muddy mess and three gleeful girls. Skipper had somehow taken the water hose from Brooke and was running around the yard spraying at random. Determined to catch the dog, Brooke was giving chase while Hailey made the attempt to head the dog off. But Skipper was faster than either girl and just as interested in keeping the hose than the girls were in getting it.

Only Ella seemed to be staying above the fray. Instead, she stood at the door surveying the scene with typical older-sister attitude. "They're being ridiculous," she said when she spied her father.

"They're being silly," he said.

And then Skipper got too close with the hose and soaked both of them. Ella squealed, but Eric could only laugh. Truly, the water felt wonderful on this warm evening.

"Hey, girls," he called. "What if I wrestle that hose out of Skipper's mouth and set up the sprinkler? I'd say you could go put your swimsuits on, but since you're already soaked there's probably no need to change."

Eric retrieved his watch and cell phone and brought them into the kitchen then kicked off his shoes, went outside and yanked the hose from the reluctant dog. Wet as he already was, there was no need for him to change out of his office clothes, either.

A few minutes later he'd set the sprinkler to the highest speed and had three happy girls and one goofy dog racing through the geysers of water. Sitting back in the lawn chair in the shade, Eric had as much fun watching the girls as they did running about.

When his growling belly could take it no more, Eric gave the five-minute warning. A chorus of complaints went up. Eric then rose and went over to the hose to turn off the water.

"Might want to think about your response to my five-minute warning next time," he said gently but firmly. "Now stay right where you are until I can get enough towels to dry you off."

He went inside to grab a stack of towels then took the teetering mound out to sit them on the chair. One by one he dispensed towels to the girls and then, with the stack that remained, he dried off the dog. Finally, he used the last towel to dry himself off as best he could.

"All right, girls," Eric said as he tossed the towel over his shoulder. "Go get into clean clothes. Leave your wet clothes in the hamper in the laundry room and be sure you comb the tangles out of your hair. Ella or Hailey, please be sure Brooke has help if she needs it."

"I can do it by myself," Brooke protested.

Eric gave his youngest daughter a kiss on the cheek. "Of course you can, sweetheart. But if you need a little help, say if your arm gets tired of combing or something like that, then your sisters can help, right, girls?"

"Right, Daddy," the older two said in unison as they followed their baby sister inside.

"Come on, Brookie," he heard Ella say as the trio disappeared down the hall toward their bedrooms. "Let's pick out something pretty to put on then you can show me how to throw wet clothes into the hamper without getting any mess on the floor."

Eric's smile was bittersweet. What a little lady Ella was becoming. At almost ten, she was growing up far too fast. And Hailey followed close behind. Where had the time gone?

He stepped inside and allowed the dog, now only slightly damp, to dart inside. While Skipper raced about like a fool, Eric padded to the kitchen to find something to feed the hungry masses he knew would come racing in demanding dinner soon enough.

Opening the fridge, he found a chips-and-chicken casserole that Mom had left along with a note telling him how to heat it. Eric turned the oven to three hundred and fifty degrees then leaned against the counter and waited for the preheat light to come on.

Faint giggles and snatches of conversation drifted across the kitchen from the direction of the girls' room. Eric closed his eyes to better hear their chatter. Hailey was talking about combs, and Brooke was singing, though the words made no sense. Just another night, and yet Eric felt acutely aware of his blessings at that moment.

And acutely aware of how very little he deserved them.

Especially given his behavior toward Amy Spencer. After an enjoyable visit, he'd practically run away like a fool only to treat her as if the whole thing was her fault when he saw her Monday morning. And on top of it all, he'd tried to be clever by asking her about her book.

If only he'd just kept his mouth shut. Or, better yet, had apologized to her in front of the rest of the staff as he'd intended to do.

But instead of the right words coming out, he'd only made things worse.

He owed her an apology.

But maybe staying away and keeping his mouth shut was the better option. Or was it the coward's way out?

A sharp, piercing beep blared through his thoughts and caused Eric's eyes to fly open. The oven's preheat light was on. He shoved the casserole in and set the timer then went to find dry clothes of his own.

Dinner came soon after and then the bed-time ritual. As he'd hoped, the backyard fun caused the girls' eyes to close far earlier than usual. The sun had barely set before Eric found the house quiet.

Eric reached for the remote then thought better of it once he noted the time. Barely past nine. Not too late to call Amy.

He found her number in his phone then moved to the sofa to get comfortable before pressing dial. Skipper joined him, laying his big head in Eric's lap as the phone rang once. Amy picked up on the fourth ring. By then Eric had given up and was about to end the call.

"I didn't think you'd answer," he said.

"Hello, Dr. Wilson" came her icy response. "Is something wrong at the clinic?"

Skipper lifted dark eyes to stare at him. Eric scratched the big dog behind one ear as he said, "I'm sorry."

"For what?" she said. "Not saying hello? You're forgiven."

"No, for..." What? What could he tell her? For letting his feelings about the guilty state of his bachelorhood cause him to behave like a fool?

"I'm sorry I bothered you tonight, Amy," Eric finally said.

"All right," Amy said slowly.

Silence settled between them as Eric continued to scratch the dog's head. "Well, all right, then," he said. "See you tomorrow."

"Yes, tomorrow." Her voice was soft, almost wistful. Or maybe he only heard what he wanted to hear.

"Amy," he said quickly. "What are you reading?"

Her chuckle was soft, sweet. "Something that isn't scary," she said.

Eric grinned and shifted the phone to the other hand. When he didn't immediately respond, Amy added, "Good night, Eric."

And then she hung up.

Amy set the phone down and reached for the book on her bedside table. She'd managed to turn three pages before she realized she hadn't read a word. Going to bed absurdly early had never been her preference, but tonight she'd arrived home bone-weary and not the least bit hungry.

Now, however, her stomach growled and her eyes refused to close. Perhaps some chamomile tea and a few strawberries sliced and dusted with sugar might do the trick. For this, Amy padded downstairs and found the fruit then set about making her snack.

When she returned to bed some twenty minutes later, she rolled over onto her side and lifted the sash on the window until the cool sea breeze washed over her. Lying beneath the low raftered ceiling in the dark, the years fell away and she was a little girl again.

With the stars twinkling over the water, Amy drifted off to sleep. And as she slept, she dreamed.

Of Eric.

When she stepped through the back door of the clinic the next morning, Amy was prepared for whatever she'd get from the other ladies. Bloom where she was planted, that was her plan.

But to her surprise, Dee had called in sick

and Nancy was on the phone taking messages. Cassie Jo had not yet arrived.

When Nancy spied Amy, she hung up and shook her head. "Want to give this message thing a try, Amy?" she asked. "Apparently I'm much better at helping the doctor stitch up patients than I am at setting up his calendar."

Cassie Jo popped in before the door shut and slipped past with a grin. "Good morning, ladies," she said as she hurried down the hall then, a moment later, reappeared minus her lunch bag and soda.

Amy slipped into the seat Nancy had just vacated and reached for the message pad. Written across the top was the number to dial for access to the voice mail and the code to get in for messages.

"Where's Dee?" Cassie Jo said as she paused at the door to the grooming room.

"Sick today," Nancy said as she gathered up the lab axes and took them to her office.

"So it's just us?" She smiled. "Let me know if you need anything, Amy."

"Thanks." She picked up the phone then set it down again and called Cassie Jo. When the groomer returned to the door, Amy said, "About yesterday…"

Cassie Jo lifted her hand as she shook her head. "Nothing to talk about, right?" She punctuated the question with a wink. "Today's a new day."

"Yes," Amy said slowly, "it is."

She returned to her work with a smile. If Cassie Jo wasn't intent on talking about the situation with Eric, and Nancy was too busy, today might be a good day, after all. That is, depending on how Eric behaved when he arrived.

Amy had finished taking the messages and was working on the file list when she spied the familiar truck pull into the parking lot. When Eric walked in, she offered a polite greeting then went back to her task.

"Could I see you in my office, Amy?"

She looked up to see Eric's expression, something between demanding and hopeful, and her heart inexplicably soared. "Yes, of course. Should I bring my notepad?" she added in case their discussion was to be business only.

"No," he said. "That won't be necessary."

"All right," she said with a smile as she followed him down the hall to his office. When he'd seated himself behind the desk, he gestured to the empty chair. Amy complied then sat very still and waited for him to speak first.

Eric wore a shirt of the same coffee-brown as his eyes and trousers a shade darker. He tugged on a shirt cuff, and she noted he wore gold cuff links. As he rested his elbows on his desk, Eric's expression went neutral. A moment later, he lifted his gaze to collide with hers.

"Is something wrong?" she managed though her heart thudded against her chest. "Have I said or done something…"

Amy let the remainder of her statement hang between them unsaid. Taking a deep breath, she let it out slowly and willed her pulse to stop racing.

The phone rang and Amy jumped up. "I should grab that."

"No," he said sharply. "Leave it."

"With Dee out it will likely go to voice mail. Is that all right?"

Eric sighed. "Things are getting complicated," he said. "And I'm wondering something."

Complicated? She shifted positions and rested her hands in her lap. "What's that?"

"Will you be staying much longer?" He leaned back in the chair as if waiting for an answer.

"I...I don't know."

"I see." He shrugged. "Dee's got a sick child so she's taken the remainder of the week off. Since we're not at full staff, we won't have our usual lunch meeting today. So, why don't we revisit this topic at next week's staff meeting?"

"Topic?" She shook her head. "What topic?"

His brows rose. "Your departure date," he said.

"My..."

"Departure," Eric supplied. "As I said, things are getting complicated."

Her heart sank. "I see."

# *Chapter Eleven*

"All right, girls," Eric said. "Who remembers what the rules are?"

"I do, I do," Hailey said while Brooke echoed her. Ella merely stared as if the fact he'd even asked was silly.

"All right. Let's say it together." He paused to help Brooke with her seat belt. "First rule of sailing is…"

"Always listen to the captain," they said in unison.

Eric nodded as he stabbed the key into the ignition and the truck's engine cranked to life. "And who is the captain?"

"You are, Daddy," again they said together.

"Very good." He shifted into Reverse and

pulled out of the driveway then headed toward Main Street. "All right. Second rule of sailing is..."

"Always wear your life jacket," the girls said.

"And how should your jacket fit, Ella?"

His eldest—so much a carbon copy of Christy that it sometimes took his breath away—smiled. "Tight."

"That's right." Eric glanced in the rearview mirror at his middle child. "And why, Hailey?"

"Because," Hailey said, her straw-colored brows lifted, "if it's too loose it will slip off and float away if we fall into the water."

"Ask me something, Daddy," Brooke complained.

"All right," he said. "When do we take off our life jackets?"

She chewed her lip and worried with the trip on her swimsuit for a moment as if deep in thought. Finally her gaze met his in the rearview mirror. "When Daddy says so."

"Very good, Brookie!" he exclaimed.

The lone traffic light on Main Street between his house and the beach turned red, and Eric slowed the truck to a stop. "All right, girls, what's the third rule of sailing?"

As they began to recite what they'd been practicing all week, Eric's mind wandered. The girls knew this. He'd been teaching them about sailing practically from the cradle. His knowledge of sailing had been passed down from father to son, and now father to daughters. Should a sailor choose to ignore that knowledge, great harm might come.

Riley had said much the same thing about life this morning at the Starting Over meeting. How the Lord can guide people but what they do with the knowledge is up to them. They make the choice.

And their choices always have consequences.

All of this had been easy to hear and easier to agree with. Then came the difficult part. The part where Riley said that each man in the group had a choice to decide how he would live his life from that moment out. Whether he'd be marked by death or made better by it. Whether he was holding on to the hurt and letting the label of *widower* define him or allowing God to show him what came next.

Eric almost got up and walked out when Riley made that statement, and he could tell from the expressions around him that he wasn't the only one who'd felt that way. He'd had no choice in the matter. Death had come to the Wilson household in spite of all actions and prayers to the contrary. And like it or not, he *was* a widower. Whether that defined him, Eric wasn't sure. But by definition, that's what he was.

Sometime in the past four years, he'd made peace with the fact that God had allowed this awful thing. What he hadn't figured out was what to do about it.

*Everything feels so temporary. As if I'm waiting on God to tell me what to do next.*

Amy had said those words at the Pizza Palace, and at the time he hadn't connected her struggle to his. Hadn't realized that, strangely, he was much like her.

The idea didn't set well.

"Daddy, you're not listening," Brooke whined. "Did we say them right or not?"

With a roll of his shoulders, Eric shook off the burden of this thoughts. "I'm sorry, sweetheart. Why don't we start over with the first one?"

A chorus of complaints rose but Eric waved them away. "Look," he said. "There's the beach and the sailboat's docked just down there. Can you say them all before I park the truck?"

"Always listen to the captain" was the only one he could understand. After that the girls spoke so fast that it all sounded like gibberish. By the time he'd found a parking space at the marina, they had given up on finishing the list and were giggling so hard they could hardly speak.

"All right, you silly girls," he said in a mock-pirate's voice as he unbuckled his seat belt. "Single file and watch your step. Argh! Anyone who doesn't listen walks the plank."

Brooke jumped out last, landing first in his arms and then feetfirst on the pavement. "Where's the plank, Daddy?" she said as her gaze scanned the perimeter.

"There's no plank, silly," Ella said as she settled her beach towel over her shoulders. "'Cept for the plank in our eyes."

"I got no plank in my eye, Ella," Brooke said. "Take that back."

"Won't," Ella stated firmly. "Miss Becky told us in Sunday-school that it says in the Bible we all have a plank in our eye."

"Does not," Brooke said while Hailey seemed more interested in a pair of gulls that were fighting for supremacy on a nearby buoy.

"Actually, Brookie," Eric said, "it does. And did she tell you what that meant, Ella?"

Ella nodded. "It means that before I tell someone what their little problem is, I should think about what my big one is. Because sometimes we can't see our own big ole plank but we can see the little speck in someone else's eye."

"That's very good," Eric said as he clicked the lock then went around to the back of the truck to retrieve the picnic basket. "And a good lesson for all of us."

Brooke motioned for him to pick her up, so he handed the basket to Ella. After climbing into his arms, Brooke put her palms on his cheeks and leaned close until they were nose to nose. "Where's yours, Daddy?"

"My what?"

"Your plank." His vision was now completely filled with the blurry image of his five-year-old's face. "I can't see it."

Eric's heart sank as he thought of how he'd treated Amy. *But I can.*

"Are we going sailing or not?" Hailey demanded. "'Cause it's hot out here and I want to feed the gulls if we're just gonna stand around and talk about planks and stuff."

"No more standing around," Eric said as he set Brooke down and once again shook off the uncomfortable thought. "We're going to go sailing. Now, single file, girls, and off we go."

After donning life vests and enduring a check of their appropriate fit, the girls were happy to watch Eric cast off. This they expressed in a series of loud squeals and giggles as the vessel lurched into motion.

"Hold on now until we get out past the swells," he said. "Remember, it might be bumpy for a few minutes, but there's a picnic at the end of the ride."

The girls obeyed and, by the time they dropped anchor at Sand Island, they'd proven themselves champion sailors. With the sun just far enough to the west and the breeze blowing enough to be comfortable, Eric inflated the small raft then set the picnic basket inside along with their beach towels.

"Everyone into the raft," he said. "Or swim it if you want to."

Of course, all three dived into the warm Gulf and swam the few yards to shore. Not surprisingly given her strength as a swimmer, Ella reached the sandy beach first with Hailey a heartbeat behind. Brooke rolled onto the sand in dramatic fashion then giggled when Eric reached them with the raft.

"That was fun, Daddy."

"Yes, it was," he said. "So how about we have our picnic now?"

The girls made short work of spreading their beach towels together to make a place to put the picnic basket. A few minutes later, they were enjoying the bounteous feast he'd purchased at the Cluck-N-Chicken on the way home from Starting Over.

"Hey, Daddy," Brooke said. "I can see our truck." She pointed toward the marina parking lot. "It looks little."

"It does," he agreed as he followed the direction of her gaze.

"And I can see the church." Hailey pointed to the stately spire.

"I can see Amy's house." Ella pointed to the cottage, and Eric's heart lurched.

"Where?" Brooke said.

While Ella pointed out the cottage with the picket fence, Eric set his plate aside. "Ella, how do you know where Amy lives?"

She shrugged. "'Cause Grammy showed us when we went to the beach last Saturday. We would've gone to say hi but Miss Amy wasn't home."

"I see." Definitely a topic to take up with his mother at the next opportunity.

"We like her, Daddy," Brooke said. "Why can't she be your new wife?"

"My new wife?" he sputtered. "Brooke, I thought you understood when we had our little talk about you three deciding to call the newspaper. If I decide to find another wife, I do not need your help. Nor do you get to say who or when that is." He lightened his expression and his tone. "Got it, girlie?" Eric said as he ruffled Brooke's hair.

Hailey touched his arm, and he turned to stare into wide blue eyes. Christy's eyes.

"We do like her, Daddy," she said. "And she likes us."

What to say? "Well, of course she does," he managed. "You're wonderful girls." A pause. "At least when you're not trying to be Daddy's little matchmakers."

He reached for Hailey and tickled her then Brooke and Ella joined in until they were all lying in the sun laughing. Thankfully the girls moved on to other subjects and left Amy Spencer out of their conversation for the remainder of the afternoon. By the time they reached dry land, with the sun hanging midway toward the horizon, Eric decided he hadn't laughed so much in years.

Nor could he recall a better day in a very long time.

If only he'd thought to bring his camera. *Next time.*

"All right," he said as he finished securing the vessel. "Ella, you get the picnic basket. Hailey, you're on beach-towel duty. Grab the bag of wet towels and leave the dry ones on board."

"For next time?" she asked with a broad grin.

Eric straightened to slip into his T-shirt. "Yes, for next time."

"Yay for next time," Brooke said. "But what's my job?"

"Your job," he said, "is to lead the way. Onward," he said. And off she went, pressing past Ella and Hailey to march toward the truck.

"Stop before you get to the parking lot," he called, and she did. Right there on the dock. Ella ran into her first with Hailey stopping just short of the collision.

"He said before the parking lot," Ella complained as she climbed to her feet and surveyed the contents of the basket, now lying on the walkway. "Why did you stop now?"

Brooke stuck her lower lip out. "It is before the parking lot, dummy."

"Brooke Wilson, you do not call your sister names. Apologize this instant and then help her pick up the mess."

She did, albeit grudgingly. By the time they'd reached the truck, however, his youngest daughter was back to her usual bubbly self.

"Look, Daddy," she said as she stood in the truck bed while Eric arranged the basket and bag of towels so they wouldn't move while he drove.

"What is it, Brookie?"

"It's Amy's house. I can see it. And she's playing in the sprinkler."

Eric chuckled and the image of Amy dashing about like his daughters had just days ago. "I highly doubt that, Brooke."

"It's true," she insisted. "Look."

Hailey climbed up beside her baby sister and craned her neck in the direction of the Spencer home. "She's right, Daddy."

Now it was Ella's turn. "Daddy," she said when she'd joined her sisters. "She is right."

"Can we go see?" Brooke said.

"Yes, Daddy, can we?" Hailey echoed.

He waited for Ella's addition to the requests. When she said nothing, he glanced over at his daughter, who was intently studying something, presumably Amy. Jumping around in the water. On a summer afternoon.

"In the truck, girls," Eric said as he tried not to think any further on the image. "First one buckled up gets to choose the ice cream at Dairy Barn after dinner tonight."

There was a mad scramble for places, and to Eric's surprise, this time Brooke won. When he climbed into the driver's seat, she offered a triumphant grin. "Well done, sweetheart," he told her. "And good job to the rest of my crew." This he said in his pirate voice.

"Daddy, you're silly," Ella said.

"Amy's silly, too," Brooke declared.

"What makes you say that?" Eric asked then wished he hadn't, for the question, asked to Brooke, prompted a conversation between the three girls whereby Amy Spencer was not only praised but practically revered.

In the midst of all this praise for Amy, Eric remembered he needed to call his mother. "All right. Hold it down," he said as he reached for his phone. A few minutes later, he'd managed to convince Mom that he and the girls had returned in one piece with nothing but fun to show for their day.

"Tell Grammy she needs to go next time," Hailey said.

When Eric relayed the message, his mother said, "I think I just might. It sounds like fun."

After hanging up the call, Eric stuck the phone in his pocket and turned the car toward the parking-lot entrance to Vine Street. To his surprise, when he looked to the right, he saw what appeared to be streams of water dancing across Vine Street in front of the Spencer home two blocks away.

"See," Brooke said. "I told you she was playing in the sprinkler."

"More like watering her garden," Eric muttered.

"Let's go see," Hailey shouted, and the other two echoed her with shouts of agreement.

The last thing Eric wanted, however, was to see Amy today. Or any day. Because the more he thought of Amy, the more he decided he was going to have to make up his mind how to deal with her.

At least as long as she remained in Vine Beach.

The thought occurred that maybe she wouldn't be here long. After all, she'd told him she felt that remaining at her grandmother's home was only temporary.

"Come on, Daddy. Just drive by."

He looked in the rearview mirror at Brooke's pleading expression. "And she is playing in the sprinkler. I saw it."

"Brooke," he said in a warning voice. "You didn't. Maybe you saw her watering the garden."

"No."

He knew that tone. Had seen that expression. If he didn't prove her wrong, Eric knew he'd never hear the end of it.

"All right," he said. "Let's go have a look, shall we? If you're right, I'll—"

"You'll what, Daddy?" Ella asked, her smirk telling Eric she didn't much believe that they would benefit from whatever he agreed to do.

What could happen? He knew he was right. So he thought of the most outlandish thing he could do. "I know. If you're right, I will stop the truck and let you all play along with her."

Another round of cheers and they were off. He turned right onto Vine Street then drove up one block until he neared the Spencer cottage. Plumes of water cascaded over the picket fence and glistened on the leaves of the shrubs.

"See," he said as he slowed the truck. "She's just…"

Then he spied Amy Spencer standing fully dressed in the middle of the flowing water, her hair hanging in a soggy ponytail down her back. A horn honked, and Eric pulled over to allow the faster moving vehicle to pass.

"I told you, Daddy," Brooke said.

"But how did you know?" The question was rhetorical, for now the dilemma was what he'd say when he pulled the truck up at the Spencer home and invited his daughters for a sprinkler party.

# Chapter Twelve

As of yesterday the silence from prospective employers was deafening. Either Amy needed to consider the fact that the Lord might be asking her to stay in Vine Beach or she needed to send out another set of résumés to employers.

Rather than decide immediately, Amy had grabbed her gardening gloves and gone outside where the afternoon was warm and the water had felt heavenly sluicing off her shoulders and dripping from her ponytail.

While the grass was only slightly parched, she had needed a swim, just to cool off a bit. But as inviting as the ocean across Vine Street looked, Amy had known she'd never get to the repairs on the front stair rail if she gave in and went over to play in the waves.

So she pressed on and moved from one garden task to the next, sipping water as she felt the need. Finally, with the sun about midway toward the horizon, she had been unable to stand the heat anymore. Amy had reached for her thermos of water and poured it over her head. The water felt so good that she considered going into the kitchen for more.

But she was already wet. So she decided to finish the chores and to treat herself to a long soak in the tub. Somewhere between weeding the walk and washing out the birdbath, she had decided that the grass was parched, and the sprinkler needed to come out.

She had found several sprinklers in the garden shed, finally choosing a yellow whirly-bird type that easily fit on the long green water hose. Positioning the sprinkler just right, she had walked to the faucet and turned the water on full force. Before long, the grass was glistening and the flowers were dancing beneath the water drops.

And she was hot as ever.

Amy had then edged around the perimeter

of the water's circle, slipping her sneakers off as she reached the gravel path. The day was still not done, but she needed time to sit in the shade and rest.

Just for a minute.

So she had made her way to the swing where the roses had not yet been watered. Resting in the rose-scented shade felt heavenly. But when she had pushed the swing just far enough at just the right time, the water from the sprinkler splashed her toes.

And that had been heavenly, too.

Not at all complicated. Amy had frowned at the reminder of what Eric had said. Things were getting complicated.

Only because he had made them that way.

Another well-timed arc of the swing, and Amy had managed to wet her legs all the way to the knees. With her hair still damp from the thermos of water and her legs dripping from the knees down, she could find no excuse to remain on the swing the next time the pulse of water came around.

Jumping directly into the stream of water had made her laugh. So she had done it again.

And again.

Until she realized she'd now soaked herself through and probably looked like a fool to anyone driving slow enough down Vine Street to notice. Of course, no one drove slowly down the beach road anymore. It was practically a racetrack during most of the day.

That is, when there were any cars at all.

So Amy jumped again, and her feet landed on the soggy grass with a splat. Mrs. King's orange-and-black cat peered at her from the safety of the fence next door with a look of disgust.

Or maybe the shifty feline was watching the beautiful monarch butterfly that flitted in and out of the streams of water, never getting splashed nor slowing down.

"Amy," a child's voice called, and she turned to see a truck slowing down on the eastbound side of Vine Street.

Eric's truck. Filled with Eric and his daughters.

Amy froze. Too late. They must have seen her.

And then the truck made a U-turn and came back. To pull into the driveway.

She groaned even as she felt like the biggest

idiot in Vine Beach. With what little dignity she had left, Amy squared her shoulders and straightened her spine then tromped through the sprinkler's spray to the fence.

Three smiling girls and one less-than-amused dad stared back through the open windows of the truck. "Hi," she said as casually as she could manage despite the water dripping off her nose.

"Amy!" A chorus rang out from the truck. Eric was not among that chorus.

"What are you girls doing here?" she asked, studiously ignoring their driver.

"We went sailing." This from Brooke whose gap-toothed grin was absolutely adorable. "And then we had a picnic and went sailing again. And Daddy talked like a pirate."

"Did he?" Despite herself, Amy glanced at Eric, who cringed. "I don't think I've ever heard your daddy talk like a pirate."

One dark brow lifted and he almost looked amused. Almost, but not quite. "And I don't think I've ever seen any of my staff from the vet clinic dancing around barefoot in a sprinkler."

Her embarrassment fading, Amy grinned.

"Well, I guess it was time, then. Now, you have me at an advantage, Dr. Wilson. You've seen me dance, but I haven't heard you speak pirate."

"And you won't," he said firmly.

"Then I guess I'll just have to lodge a protest."

He shrugged. "Get in line. I've got three girls ahead of you."

Amy looked at the now-solemn faces. "What's wrong?"

"I'm mad at Daddy," Brooke said. "He didn't do what he said."

"I see," Amy said.

"We came to play in the sprinkler with you," Brooke continued. "But now Daddy says we can't."

"Oh?" She made a valiant attempt at covering her surprise as she returned her attention to Eric. "Do you have to be somewhere?" Amy gestured to the still-spinning sprinkler. "Because if you've got the time to talk like a pirate, I've got the time to listen."

A direct use of his statement to her the last time he sat in his truck in front of her house.

Not that he'd likely remember, what with his grumpy attitude last week.

Whether he recalled making the statement or not was not immediately evident. However, it was quickly evident that the girls got the final say in whether they would stay.

"But you'll have to ride home in wet clothes. All our beach towels are soaked and full of sand."

"I don't mind loaning you a few," Amy said sweetly. "I don't think that would be too complicated, do you?"

An awareness of her meaning passed between them, and Eric had the decency to duck his head. When he met her gaze again, his expression had softened.

"Daddy, pleeeeaaaase!" Hailey said.

"Yeah, Daddy, you said!"

Finally he appeared to have had enough. Raising his hand, he silenced the tiny mob then, slowly, he returned his attention to Amy. "We've imposed on your..." He shook his head. "Your dancing or whatever it was you were doing."

"It was complicated," she said, enjoying his wince at the jab a bit too much. "Mostly watering the grass. And me," Amy amended. "See, I'd been working in the yard all day and was about to tackle that leaning porch rail when I decided I needed to cool off first."

A nod and then he swiveled to face the girls. In profile he was every bit as handsome as when he gave her that frustrated stare.

"Maybe for a few minutes," he grumbled. "But just five or ten minutes. No more. Understand?" And then he added a piratelike "Arrrrgh!"

A chorus of "Yes, Daddy" went around the backseat of the truck and then the girls piled out and ran around to race inside the fence. Their father moved at a considerably slower pace as he stepped out of the truck and palmed the keys.

When he moved around the truck, Amy could see that Eric wore a gray T-shirt with Texas Aggie Football emblazoned across the front in maroon letters and a pair of black board shorts that hung just above the knee. A slight dusting of red across his nose and cheeks gave evidence that he'd been out in the sun recently.

They gazes met over the fence. Again, he almost smiled. "What?" she dared ask.

He shrugged. "Nothing."

"Well, all right, then." Amy turned her back on him to walk around the edge of the circle of water and meet the girls. Hugging each one at least twice, she gestured to the sprinkler. "Go on and have fun," she said.

While the two older girls ran off to play, Brooke lagged behind. She grasped Amy's hand and looked up at her with big blue eyes fringed with thick black lashes. "Aren't you going to dance in the water, too?"

Amy knelt down to get on eye level with the little girl. "Actually, I'm kind of tired right now. I thought I might go ahead and finish my chores while you and your sisters and daddy enjoy the sprinkler. Is that okay?"

Brooke appeared to be considering the question. Then Hailey called Brooke's name, and she was off to join them. The trio danced and jumped, squealed and laughed. Amy stood and watched, struck by the sweetness of the moment.

Out of the corner of her eye, Amy saw Eric

approach. "Don't let them fool you," he said when he stopped beside her.

Amy slid him a sideways glance. "What do you mean?"

"They're not always this loud."

As if they'd heard, the volume level went up, causing the Kings' cat to flee. The butterfly, however, continued to flit about, though keeping a safe distance from the chaos.

"They're just being little girls," Amy said in their defense. "And little girls are noisy." A pause. "But then, I would imagine, so are little boys."

"My mother would have plenty to say on that." His chuckle was soft and low. "And does, regularly. She's particularly fond of reminding me of all the things my brother and I did just about the time I'm about to go fuss at one of the girls."

"You're lucky to have her."

He nodded. "I am. She's made things much less..."

"Complicated?" Amy offered innocently.

Eric turned to her, arms crossed. "Can we supervise these girls from the porch?"

"Yes," she said, though she felt much more

comfortable standing with him out here than sitting with him up there. "We can see them just fine from up there."

He nodded and moved toward the porch, leaving Amy to follow. He paused only long enough to notice the hammer and nails sitting on the step. "It's going to need more than that," he said. "I'll bring the right tools over tomorrow after church."

A statement, not a question, and thus no reason for Amy to respond. She picked up her things and carried them up onto the porch, depositing the hammer on the floor outside the door and the nails on the table between the rockers.

Eric moved toward the far end of the porch and leaned on the rail, his attention focused on the girls. Slowly he turned his head. As their gazes collided, Amy felt suddenly aware that her clothing, thankfully dark and loosely fitting, was soaked.

She looked down and tugged on her shorts. "Would you excuse me a minute?" Before he could respond, Amy hurried inside and raced up the narrow stairs to her bedroom. A few minutes later, her hair freshly bundled into a ponytail and wearing a pale yellow sundress, Amy walked downstairs to the screen door and looked out.

Eric had moved both rockers down to the end of the porch nearest the girls. He leaned against the back of one, apparently watching his daughters. And smiling.

He had such a nice smile.

Abruptly he looked in her direction. "Amy?" he said

"Yes, I'm here. Can I get you some tea?" she asked.

"No, thank you." The smile broadened. "You look nice," he said. "But you didn't have to change on my behalf. I'm afraid I'm still wearing the clothes I went sailing in." A chuckle. "And swimming, though it was only the few yards between the boat and Sand Island."

"You went to Sand Island?" She moved toward him, allowing the door to slam behind her. "I can see it from the window in my bedroom. I always wondered what it was like," Amy said as she settled in the rocker beside him.

"Well," Eric said with a chuckle. "It's sandy."

"Hence the name," she supplied.

"Yes, and the beach is nice. Decent shells there because they don't get picked over like they do on Vine Beach. And the tide's not bad. The girls were able to play in the water without me having to worry too much." He shrugged. "It's a great place for a picnic. Dad used to take us boys out there when we were kids."

Amy looked down at the girls, who were now making a vain attempt at chasing the butterfly. "I'm sure your girls loved it."

"They did. You should go."

"No, that's probably not a good idea."

He seemed confused by her statement then, slowly, he nodded. Brooke called her name and she rose to wave at the five-year-old.

The chair creaked, drawing Amy's attention. "Look, I need to apologize."

Several responses came to mind. Amy said none of them as she took her seat once more.

"First for the way I bolted out of here the other day." He leaned forward and rested his elbows on his knees, his focus on the porch floor. Slowly he looked over at her. "I had a great time. Really great." Eric let out a long breath. "Too great, I guess."

Amy leaned her head against the back of the rocker and rested her hands in her lap. "I don't know what you mean. Is that bad?"

"No, it's…"

"Complicated?" she offered.

"Yeah. Complicated." Eric straightened and gripped the arms of the rocker. "See, I haven't enjoyed myself like that in a long time." He paused. "Years."

Amy sat very still while the sound of crashing waves and giggling girls swirled around them. "And you felt guilty."

He nodded.

She sighed. "That is complicated."

"It is." Eric released his grip on the chair. "You said something at the Pizza Palace. About wondering why everything feels so temporary. As if you were waiting on God to tell you what to do next."

"You remembered."

"Because I understand that feeling more than you know." A delivery truck roared past on Vine Street, interrupting their conversation. "Yours is location. Mine's situation. But it's all the same, isn't it?"

Amy began to rock, her fingers tracing a path across the worn wood of the rocker's arm. "I suppose it is. But what's the answer? I still don't know." She paused. "Maybe everything is temporary. Maybe we're losing sight of the moment if we're worrying too much about the future."

"Or the past," he said softly.

She reached across the space between them to press her palm to his shoulder. "I've never experienced what you have. The loss of someone you love? I can't imagine what it must be…" Amy shook her head. "Anyway, I just wish I had some sort of wisdom to offer. Something to make it better."

She felt his sigh rather than heard it. Slowly Amy removed her hand from his shoulder and rested it once again in her lap, her palm warm from the contact.

"You do make it better," he said. "And that's the most complicated part of all."

"Daddy," Ella called.

He looked away slowly, reluctantly. "What is it, sweetheart?"

"We're hungry. Can we go get ice cream now?"

"Yeah, Daddy," Brooke said. "And remember, I get to pick."

Another sigh and Eric rose. "Looks like I need to trouble you for those towels now."

She nodded and went inside to retrieve three fluffy blue beach towels. By the time she returned to the porch, she brought a plan, as well.

"You know, Eric, I was going to make a salad. I'd love it if you and the girls would join me." She handed him the towels.

He thought a moment then nodded. "The girls would like that," he said. "And a much better dinner than ice cream."

"Well, I don't know about that," Amy teased. "As a single woman I've had dessert for dinner on more than one occasion. Though I don't advocate it for more than special occasions."

Eric laughed. "All right. Let me rephrase that. Salad will be a much more nutritious meal."

"Agreed," she said as she rose. "I'll get the basket and my gardening gloves. Do you dare go down there with the girls and turn off the water or shall I?"

"I'll do it. You're already dressed in dry clothes." He gave her a swift but appraising glance. "You look really nice, by the way."

"Thank you."

"The hose is attached to the faucet on the wall behind the swing. You can go through the house and out the back door if you'd like to avoid the girls. Or you can brave the water and sprint across the front yard."

"Not much of a choice there," he said as he stood. "I haven't sprinted in a very long time." He leaned over the rail and spied the girls. "I'm going to turn off the water now, girls," he said to a chorus of groans. "Hey, if you're hungry, you can't eat and play in the water at the same time, can you?"

Grudging agreement rose. "All right," he said to them. "Amy and I will be down in a minute to tell you about what we're doing for dinner."

"Rocky road," Brooke called.

"You don't even know what that is, Brooke Wilson," Eric called. "And no, we aren't having ice cream for dinner." He turned to

Amy. "And for the record, we never were. I planned to take them to the grocery store for ice cream that we could bring home and have for dessert after I warmed up the leftovers from last night's casserole."

"You make casseroles? I'm impressed."

Eric shook his head. "Don't be. I am the chief recipient of my mother's handiwork. She loves nothing better than finding casserole recipes and trying them out on the girls and me."

"I see." She gestured to the door. "Shall we?" Amy opened the screen door and led Eric inside. Never a large place by anyone's standards, the room seemed to shrink with Eric Wilson standing in it. "This way."

He followed her through the parlor and into the kitchen. "It smells great in here."

Amy took a deep breath. "That's the roses." She pointed to the table where a vase filled to overflowing with Nana's pink cabbage roses awaited their trip to the assisted-living facility tomorrow afternoon.

"Sure beats a spice candle," he said, and she recalled the lovely scent of spice that permeated his kitchen.

"With Nana's flower garden, I find I don't need candles." She walked to the back door and stepped out onto the little porch. "See over there?" Amy said. "That's the faucet. Turn it to the left to shut it off."

His brow wrinkled. "Shouldn't it be to the right? My dad always taught me 'Righty tighty, lefty loosey.'"

Amy laughed. "Mine, too! Isn't that funny?" Then she shrugged. "I'm not sure why, but the plumbing in this place leaves something to be desired. My guess is someone hired a plumber who didn't know what he was doing. Anyway, it's all backward."

"So hot is cold and cold is hot?"

"Yes," she said, "but don't worry. Grandpa had all the fixtures changed to reflect that. When you turn on the hot, it's hot."

Eric shook his head. "You've lost me. But that's okay. I'll get that water turned off and you can get whatever it is you need to make the salad."

"It's all right here." She pointed to the potting closet. "Nana always liked having her gardening things close to the house."

She fetched what she needed and followed

Eric down the back stairs. A moment later, he'd managed to turn off the water, much to the girls' complaints.

"Towels are up on the porch," he told them as he came around the corner. "Ella, go get them and bring down enough for all three of you. When you're dry enough, come and see what Amy's going to make for us."

"Actually, you're going to help. Would you like that?"

Amid the cheering, Ella broke away to run up the stairs and retrieve the towels. She came back down and handed towels to her sisters then wrapped herself in the remaining one.

"All right," Amy said when the girls were ready. "Here's what we're going to do."

# Chapter Thirteen

It did not escape Eric's attention that he sat in the same spot he'd fled from one week ago. This time his girls were with him. Whether that made a difference or whether admitting the problem to Amy had reduced it, he couldn't say. But things were becoming far less complicated with every minute that ticked by.

And they were ticking.

The sun had set, leaving orange fingers of fiery color dancing across the waves. The porch light sent fractures of light through the prisms of glass and gave the table where they now sat a fanciful look.

The table had long ago been cleared, though

Amy refused his help with the dishes. He looked across the table where Amy was engaged in a deep philosophical conversation with Brooke regarding the finer points of slicing an apple over eating it in bites. Amy preferred slicing while Brooke liked to bite chunks. Hailey and Ella, however, were busying themselves using Amy's paper plates and several colored pens to make art for Amy's grandmother and theirs.

All three little girls—and the big girl—looked as if they could fall asleep at any moment. And Eric wasn't too far from that state himself.

"Ladies, I believe it's time to go." He looked over at Amy. "Thank you for your hospitality. But it's time we leave."

"Is it time to get ice cream?" Brooke asked.

Eric glanced at his watch. "Sweetie, it's late. Past your bedtime. We'll have to get our ice cream tomorrow."

"All right, Daddy," Brooke said, clear evidence to Eric that she was exhausted. "Carry me?" she added when he rose.

"You'll have to walk down the steps by yourself," he said to her. "Daddy's got to come back tomorrow and fix that stair rail but until then it's best that we be very careful." He looked over at Amy. "Will I see you at church tomorrow?"

"Actually, I promised my grandmother I'd attend the services at the senior center with her again this week."

*So that's where she must have been last week.* Eric nodded. "Then with your permission I'll come by sometime in the afternoon and fix this rail." He leaned close. "Without my helpers," he whispered.

"Really, Eric, it's not necessary."

He gave her an even look. "I want to do this, all right?" A pause. "I won't bother you, if that's what you were thinking. I'll bring my own tools. You wont even know I'm here."

Was it his imagination or did Amy look the slightest bit disappointed at that claim?

"Daddy," Ella said, "these are for Grammy. And here, Amy. Give these to your grammy."

"Well, I think it is necessary, Amy." He took the decorated paper plates that Ella handed him.

"Thank you, Ella," Amy said as she took the plates, and gave each girl a hug. "She will like them very much."

Eric loaded the girls in the truck then offered a wave to Amy, who remained on the porch. "Wait, Daddy!" Brooke called. "You forgot something."

He pressed on the brake and shifted the truck into Park then swiveled around to look at Brooke. "What did you forget, sweetie?"

She shook her head. "No, *you* forgot." Brooke paused to give him an I-can't-believe-you-don't-know-what-I'm-talking-about look. "Pirate talk, Daddy. You promised Amy you would talk pirate to her."

Eric sighed. Leave it to his daughters to catch him in the most ridiculous promise he'd made in ages. "Hmm, I did say *Argh,*" he said while he tried to think his way out of the dilemma. Thankfully, he spied the front door open then close behind Amy. "Oops," he said with mock dismay. "Amy's inside now. I'll have to talk pirate to her another time."

"Like tomorrow?" Ella said in a teasing tone.

"When you come see her?" This from Hailey, whose high-pitched singsong voice held more than a little enthusiasm.

"I am not coming to see her. I'm coming to fix the stairs on her grandmother's house." He turned back around and settled his seat belt comfortably around him. "And no, you may not come with me."

"But, Daddy," the trio said in unison.

"No," he said. "Remember, you're going to lunch and a movie after church with the kids from the youth group."

"But Brooke's too little to go with us," Ella protested. "She always has to leave the theater to go potty."

"Hey," Brooke said.

"It's so annoying," Hailey added.

"It might be annoying, but it's nothing different than the two of you did," he said. "And Grammy's going along as one of the chaperones, so she'll be keeping an eye on Brooke."

"And taking her to the potty a thousand times," Ella said.

"Enough, Ella. Watch how you speak about your sister or you'll find yourself home with me instead of out having fun."

"Then you couldn't go visit Amy," she said sarcastically.

Eric opened his mouth to tell her she was grounded tomorrow then decided to let it go. At almost ten, his eldest daughter was finding her place in the world. Or at least that's what his mother told him was happening. Far as he was concerned these little attitude issues, though currently few and far between, needed to be nipped in the bud before they became a real problem.

They drove home in silence, and by the time Eric pulled the truck into the garage, Ella was back to her usual happy self. After she and her sisters were asleep, Eric got ready for bed but found his thoughts refused to quiet so he could sleep. Especially thoughts of Amy Spencer.

Finally he turned on the light and folded his hands behind his head. How had things gotten so… "Complicated," he said with a sigh as he threw back the covers and put his feet on the floor. "How did that happen, Lord?"

Eric rose to pad to the kitchen for a glass of water then stopped to look out the window. The moon rode high over the treetops and illuminated the backyard with a silvery glow. Somewhere that same moonlight was covering Amy Spencer's house.

And likely she wasn't having a bit of trouble sleeping.

Skipper wandered up behind him and nudged his leg. "Hey, fella," he said as he scratched the big dog's ears. "Can't sleep, either?"

As if on cue, the spaniel lay down and rested his head on Eric's foot. "Cute," he said as he slid his foot from under the dog's snout and emptied his glass into the sink.

A piece of paper on the end of the counter caught Eric's eye and he reached for it. His ten rules for sailing, written in Ella's handwriting. He read them with a smile then returned the paper to the counter and walked back down the hall to his room.

If only there were ten rules of relationships. Or ten rules of finding a wife. Or, better yet, ten characteristics of the perfect wife. For that matter, he'd settle for ten rules for moving forward in life.

"Now's a list I could use," he said to Skipper.

And if forward meant into the arms of Amy Spencer, he'd just have to figure out how to deal with that eventuality. For though he knew he had to do something besides stay stuck, he still hadn't quite moved toward accepting it all.

Not really. In theory, maybe. But in reality? Putting someone else in Christy's place was going to take a leap of faith that he hoped he could manage when the time came. Because tonight, lying alone in his bed with their daughters sleeping down the hall, he couldn't imagine it.

But then there had been times this afternoon when he could. He had thought endlessly about his children growing up without a mother. And yet he just couldn't decide that his entire life should change.

It didn't help that the sermon the next morning at church was about embracing change. And letting God have His way even when it wasn't comfortable.

So when his mother cornered him after church to tell him she had a great idea, Eric figured he was about to be confronted with a little more change. "I thought you were supervising the youth on their movie trip."

"I am," Mom said. "So I need to make this quick. We need another sail. Just you and me and the girls." He was about to agree when she added, "And Amy."

"Amy?" Eric shook his head. "Mother, what are you up to?"

"Well, darling," she said as she touched his sleeve, "I've decided I want to give sailing a try."

He lifted a brow. "All these years and you never set foot on a sailboat for fear you'd break a nail or mess up your hair. Why now?"

"Everything in its season, Eric. I'm embracing change. Now don't make such a fuss about it."

He sighed. The correlation to today's sermon was slight at best. "All right," Eric said with as much patience as he could manage given the topic and location. "But why invite Amy?"

"I could make up some silly excuse," she said as she met his stare, "but what would be the point. I like her. The girls like her. And I think you like her, as well."

"Amy's a nice girl," he agreed.

"Great, then we'll have a nice sail next Saturday. At one."

"That's rather specific, Mother. Does this mean you've already asked her?"

"Don't be silly," she said. "That's your place. I just told her you had something important to talk to her about." A pause. "Oh, and not to make plans for Saturday at one until she spoke with you."

He laughed. "Stop teasing."

Mom affected a pout. "I assure you I'm completely serious."

Now she had his attention. And his concern. "But she wasn't at church this morning and the girls and I were at her place until late. When did you manage to tell her this?"

"Eric, really. Do you think that because I'm old I don't know how the young people communicate?" His mother paused. "I sent a text message. If I were you I'd expect a response."

He tried to decipher her statement. "If you were *me?* How can she respond to your text message on my phone?"

"No, dear," she said patiently. "She's going to respond to your text. The one I sent while you were getting the girls settled into their Sunday-school classes."

"You didn't!" He reached into his pocket and pulled out his phone. Sure enough, there was a new text, sent by him to Amy Spencer. "Mother," he managed through gritted teeth, "I cannot believe you did this."

"You always leave your phone in your

pocket. You're such a creature of habit, Eric." She grinned. "It's going to do you good to embrace change."

"Embrace change?" he sputtered. "This isn't change. It's an invasion of privacy."

"Eric, really." Mom paused to wave at an elderly couple as they exited the building then returned her attention to Eric. "It's just a sail, and you said yourself that it was a good idea to ask her. I just helped you out."

Shock rendered him momentarily speechless. "Helped me out?" he finally managed.

"Yes, dear, but there's no need to thank me. Now, I must go. The children's department director will be wondering where I went." She darted away but had the audacity to turn around to blow a kiss and then wave over her shoulder before disappearing around the corner.

Drawing in a long breath, he let it out slowly in the hopes some of his irritation would follow. It did not.

Someone clasped a hand on his shoulder, and he turned around to see Riley standing behind him. "Good sermon, wasn't it?" Riley said.

Eric dropped his phone back into his pocket

and shook his friend's hand. "Made me wonder if you and the pastor were in collusion."

"Nah," Riley said. "My guess is the Lord just wanted to get the message out and He used both of us to do it." He chuckled. "Happens like that sometimes."

They talked for a few minutes as they walked toward the parking lot. A few paces from the parking lot, an older man called Riley's name. After saying his goodbyes, Riley struck off toward the fellow, and Eric headed to the truck.

He'd just climbed in behind the wheel when his phone vibrated in his pocket. He turned his key in the ignition to allow the air-conditioning to begin cooling the interior then reached into his pocket.

One text.

From Amy Spencer.

Eric palmed the phone and leaned his head back against the headrest to let out a long breath. Slowly, he lifted the phone up to view the screen then pressed the text icon to reveal the message.

Okay.

"Okay?" He shook his head. "What does *okay* mean?"

*Okay she's free?*

*Okay she's willing to talk to me?*

*Or something else entirely?*

Eric ran his hand through his hair and contemplated the phone's screen until it went black. Then he clicked the respond key and waited until the proper screen was revealed.

How to respond?

He set the phone on the seat and swiped his palms on his pants while blaming their clamminess on the heat and humidity. When he picked up the phone again, he once again had to find the respond key. Finally, he began to type.

Look, my mother overstepped her bounds today in contacting you. She's never been one to respect boundaries. But you already know that thanks to the newspaper…

"No. Too wordy."

Shaking his head, Eric hit Delete then tried again.

I'm sure you were surprised by this text.
I know I was when my mother told me
she'd sent it. So, in light of the fact that
neither of us expected her to...

"No. Too whiny."

Once again he removed the text. This time,
before he typed, Eric set the phone aside to
figure out just how to respond. His eyes slid
shut. "What do I say, Lord?" he whispered.
"This is just too much change."

But was it? Who was he to put limits on
God?

Deep in his sleepy heart, Eric felt the
faintest beginnings of something. Might be
change, or maybe it was the leftover casserole
he ate for his midnight snack.

He lifted the phone and typed one word:
Okay.

# Chapter Fourteen

Amy took her time returning home after her lunch with Nana. Partly because she'd had such a good visit with her grandmother and partly because she wasn't quite ready to face Eric should he be making good on his promise to repair the stair rail.

When she pulled into the driveway at the cottage, Amy noted with relief that Eric's truck was not there. Jumping out, she gathered her things and let out the breath she hadn't realized she was holding.

Her phone bounced onto the ground, and Amy picked it up and stuffed it back into her purse. Odd that he had something to talk to her about and wanted to see that she was available Saturday at one.

If this was anyone else, she might assume he would be asking her out. But this was Eric. The guy who rightly characterized their relationship as complicated. Who'd told her on Friday to consider tending her resignation on the following Wednesday then showed up for dinner on Saturday.

And yet, Amy dared to consider the possibility that perhaps Eric had moved past complicated to interested. He *had* said that the fact she made him feel good was what made things so difficult. Did he now intend to ask her for a date?

A real date? Like a normal guy?

Not that she'd dated any normal guys in a very long time. And she'd never dated a normal guy with three children.

Though his girls were absolutely delightful.

Then there was the fact that she worked for him. That, however, was temporary and could change at any time. And might, depending on what she decided to do on Wednesday.

She rounded the corner then stepped over the Kings' cat to head up the walkway. Immediately she noticed that the leaning stair rail was now missing.

Carefully picking her way up the steps, Amy looked around for a note. Finding none, she thrust her hand into her purse to retrieve her keys. As she reached the bottom of the bag, her phone beeped, indicating another text.

Eric.

She stabbed the key into the lock and opened the door. Leaving the door open to allow the sea breeze to flow through the stuffy house, Amy went into the kitchen and set her purse down then leaned against the old Chambers stove and retrieved the message.

Tried to get delivery date sooner. Hope the paint matches.

"What?" She shook her head then read the message again. Again it made no sense. She typed a question mark into the box and pressed send.

Lumberyard out of treated wood in that width. Will deliver new rails on Saturday.

Couldn't find paint can in shed. Had to guess on color.

"Saturday," she said softly. "At one."

Of course. Her heart sank as she thought about the missing stair rail. This wasn't about a date at all.

The text was about the delivery of a pile of wood.

On Saturday.

At one.

She sent back a quick okay then set the phone on the counter. With a sigh, Amy kicked off her shoes then carried them up-stairs. Once she'd changed into comfortable clothes, Amy headed downstairs to pour a glass of iced tea and snag her "beach read" for a little relaxation time on the porch.

A glance outside told her she'd forgotten to put away the sprinkler, so she hurried out to roll up the hose and stow the sprinkler head in the garage. Best to keep the yard clear should Mr. King decide to come and cut the grass. While the older man was sweet and very thor-ough when he brought over his riding mower, he rarely bothered to remove any objects in the way. She'd lost several hoses and a nice pair of gardening gloves this way.

That mission accomplished, Amy straightened and looked up at the house and then over the fence in the direction of the King home. Had she heard someone calling her? A moment's wait revealed only silence, so she shrugged and went back to the kitchen.

"Time to finish this novel," she said under her breath. "And start that new one I've been dying to read."

Stuffing the phone into the pocket of her shorts, Amy held the tea glass in one hand and the book in the other as she whirled around and slammed into Eric Wilson. He caught her arms and kept her from falling backward, though the glass of tea went flying.

The shock of ice-cold liquid blended with the sight of the veterinarian was enough to render her temporarily speechless. "What in the world are you doing here?" Amy sputtered when she could manage to speak.

Eric, however, had no such trouble with his voice. He began to apologize immediately. Even as the tea was still dripping down his shirt.

"I thought you heard me calling you," he said as he swiped at the icy liquid. "You were outside. And I..." He stepped forward to reach for the dish towel, and ice cubes crunched under his feet. "Ironically, I came in to tell you that I had just noticed that your doorbell was broken. Anyway, I'm sorry."

Her shaking fingers found a fresh towel in the drawer nearest the sink and dabbed at the brown stain on her blue top. "No, it's fine," she said. "I was... That is, I didn't..." She let the hand holding the dish towel drop to her side. "Sorry, I seem to be completely out of words. I didn't expect to see you there, much less..."

"Much less blocking the door?"

Amy shook her head. "I was going to say, much less pour tea on you." She paused. "But all right, I'll take blocking the door."

Eric ducked his head then looked up to toss the towel into the sink. "We keep running into one another, don't we?" He groaned. "Sorry, that was bad, even for me."

In spite of herself, Amy began to giggle. When she met his troubled gaze and spied his tea-soaked shirt, her giggle became laughter. "I'm sorry. It's not funny." She shook her head. "That is, your joke was funny but the fact I've ruined your shirt isn't."

It was Eric's turn to shake his head. "No, it wasn't funny. And I've ruined your shirt."

"By stepping into my tea glass? Hardly." She shrugged. "Though I should probably change. Do you mind? If I go put on something less damp?"

"Sure," he said. "I'll go on out and finish what I can today on the stairs then come back when the materials are delivered."

"Yes, I got your text."

Eric made a face. "About that."

"Oh, I don't have any plans so Saturday at one will be just fine."

"But I haven't told you the details."

She shook her head. "Don't need to know. Just let me know what it costs because I insist on paying."

"Paying?" He looked perplexed. "Um, there's no cost."

"But…" Amy noted his insistent look and gestured to the hall and the stairs beyond. "Maybe we could table the discussion for later. Now if you'll excuse me I'll just go up now and…"

"Oh, right. And I'll go on out and…well… out."

When she came downstairs, Eric had changed into a black T-shirt and was hammering nails into the arm of the swing. Amy walked over to the edge of the porch and peered down. "What are you doing?" She paused. "And where'd you get the clean shirt?"

Eric rose, hammer still in hand. "Trying to see that this swing doesn't fall apart. It appears to be well loved."

"It is," Amy said.

"And as for the shirt," he said as he looked down then back at Amy, "I've been going to this men's group at the church and they play a little basketball."

She narrowed her eyes so as to better read the white letters. "Starting Over? I've never heard of it."

He shrugged. "Like I said, it's a men's group. For widowers. Riley Burkett heads it up."

"Yes, I know Mr. Burkett. He's a nice man." She paused. "Too bad about his wife."

Eric set the hammer on the swing's seat then focused his attention on Amy. "Would you have something I can oil these chains with?"

"Sure." She gestured to the house. "Be right back." Retrieving a spray can, she returned to her place on the porch. "Here, catch," Amy said.

He did and then proceeded to coat the metal chain with the lubricant. "This should help," Eric said. "At least it won't make so much noise when you're swinging." He turned to face the ocean. "Nice view from here."

"Yes," she said. "It is."

"I strengthened the bottom of the seat, as well. It was sagging a little. Figured you wanted it to last." Eric gestured to the swing. "Well, come on down and try it."

Amy smiled and did as he asked. "This is wonderful, Eric," she said as she leaned into the swing's wooden back. "And the chains aren't making all that noise." She paused. "Thank you."

"My pleasure," he said. "I'm glad you don't mind that I meddled with it."

"Actually, I was a little worried about how much longer I would have this old swing."

Amy ran her hand over the arm. "My grand-father built the arbor and hung the swing so long ago that neither Nana nor Mrs. King next door can remember when. It's nice that it will be around awhile."

She pushed back then let go, lifting her feet to set the swing in motion. Higher it went in an easy and quiet arc until her toes felt as if they could touch the sky. Only when she realized the handsome vet was watching her with far too much amusement did she allow the swing to slow to a stop.

"Oh, this is lovely," Amy said.

He gestured to the empty spot beside her. "May I?"

"Yes, of course." She scooted a bit closer to the end and braced her feet on the ground to hold the swing still while Eric settled in place.

Acutely aware of the man beside her, Amy distracted herself by looking past the picket fence to the cars passing on Vine Street and the beach beyond. Strollers and sunbathers populated the sandy shore while several dozen energetic souls swam or bounced around in clusters on rafts and floating toys. Overhead, gulls screeched, dipped and dived toward a child holding something enticing.

"Amy," he said softly.

She swiveled to face him but remained silent. He planted his feet firmly on the ground and then rested her elbows on his knees, his expression solemn.

"Something wrong?" she finally said. "If it's about the shirt I ruined with that iced tea, I'm really sorry. I—"

"No, that's not it. I don't care about that old shirt." He glanced at her over his shoulder. "What I'm concerned with is something else." He paused to let out a long breath then leaned back against the swing and crossed his arms over his chest. "That text you got this morning."

Again, she remained silent. Rather, she nodded.

"I didn't send it." He shook his head. "I might have, if given the chance, but I didn't." Eric slid her a sideways glance. "My mother did."

His pained expression baffled her. If the text was about a lumber delivery, what did it matter who sent it?

"Well," Amy said carefully, "I'm sure she meant no harm. You would have had to tell me about the lumber delivery at some point. It doesn't bother me that she handled that for you."

"Lumber delivery?" Eric shook his head. "What are you talking about?"

"Well, your first text, or rather your mother's first text, said you needed to talk to me about something important. Something happening on Saturday at one."

"Right," he said with a nod.

"And then just a little while ago you sent a text. Or was that your mother, too?"

Eric ducked his head. "No, she just sent the one. I sent the lumber one."

"Well, anyway, you sent that text telling me about the Saturday lumber delivery. Which I assumed was—"

"At one o'clock." He slapped his forehead then rose abruptly. The swing shook upon his departure. "I'm sorry, Amy. No wonder you were confused." He shrugged. "It seems as though you're the new target."

Eric looked at her as if she knew what he meant. "Oh?" was the best she could manage.

"And while I do enjoy spending time with you, I prefer that it's me who does the planning and not my mother. For the record, she stopped being my social secretary several decades ago. No, that's wrong. She never was."

She covered the beginnings of her smile by looking away. Apparently he just needed someone to vent to.

"I can ask a woman on a date if I want to." Eric came to stand between her and the roses. He was so close she had to lean back to see his face.

"Of course you can," Amy said slowly. "And apparently your mother and daughters want that for you. Maybe that's why they're working so hard to make it happen."

"Well, I can do this myself." He paused. "I'm asking you out. On a date. Will you go out with me?"

Amy jerked to attention. "On a date?" she echoed.

"Yes."

His determined look was absolutely adorable. "When?"

He glanced at his watch. "What about now?"

"Now?" She shook her head. "That's a little soon, don't you think?"

"No," he said firmly, "I don't."

"Well," Amy said as she reached to toy with the cross at her neck. "All right." She looked down at her casual outfit then over at him. "Should I go and change?"

"You might want to throw a swimsuit on under your clothes." At her surprised look, he continued. "I'm thinking of a sail. You did say you've never seen Sand Island up close. I can get the sailboat to within a few yards of shore when the tide's just right but we'll have to swim the rest of the way."

Sailboat? Her stomach turned over at the thought. And yet her pride wouldn't allow Amy to admit she had a horrible time with seasickness.

"Oh, I don't know, Eric," she said slowly, even as she took in his boyish grin and his obvious enthusiasm for the idea.

His smile fell. "Don't you want to go for a sail?"

"Well, yes, of course. A sail sounds lovely." *In theory.* "It's just that when I'm out on the water I get—"

His cell phone blared a ring that sounded like an alarm going off. Eric yanked his phone from his pocket. "I'm so sorry, but I need to get this. It's the emergency line," he said as he punched the button. "Wilson, here," he said into the phone. "Yes, fine, tell me what's wrong."

As Eric asked questions, nodding in between, Amy began to realize she was off the hook for an impromptu sail this afternoon. He gave the caller some instructions then hung up with a promise to meet at the vet clinic in a few minutes.

"I'm sorry," he said as he stuffed the phone back into his pocket. "Looks like our sail will have to wait for another day."

"I understand," she said as she rose and walked with Eric toward his truck. *And in the interim I'll be stocking up on seasickness preventatives.*

He paused at the sidewalk. "So, for the record," Eric said. "I do have a lumber delivery scheduled for Saturday, but they haven't told me the time yet. The driver's got instructions to put the lumber on the back porch if no one's here."

"All right," she said, "but I'm still going to have to protest the fact that you're paying for things that should rightly be my expense."

Eric grinned. "I anticipated that and I've worked out a payment schedule. I figure if you keep plying me with sweet tea and coconut cake we ought to be settled up in a year or two."

She laughed. "I'll see what I can do. Remember, that was my grandmother's cake."

"Well," he said slowly, "you're already ahead of things, what with the tea you poured on my shirt."

Amy cringed. "Sorry about that," she said. "But in my own defense, the last thing I figured to run into on my way to the porch was you."

"Which reminds me," he said. "I need to pick up a new doorbell for you. I'll do that tomorrow. Lunchtime maybe. Or I could call and have the lumberyard deliver one." He gave Amy a thoughtful look. "But you'd probably like to pick one out. Do you have a preference?"

"Actually, I haven't given it much thought."

"Then think about it. If you go online you'll

see there are all sorts of types." He placed his hand on her arm, and Amy's heart inexplicably lurched. "Okay, well, I've got to go. As I said, I'll get on this tomorrow."

"Eric, really, you don't have to worry about the doorbell," she said as she watched him disappear into his truck. "Or any of this other stuff. If I can't figure out how, I'm sure Mr. King would help me—"

The door shut and the engine cranked to life, ending any hope Amy might have of continuing the conversation. When her text-message notice sounded, Amy reached into her pocket for her phone. It was Eric.

She looked up to shake her head at him, but he was still out of her line of vision. Amy pressed the text icon and the screen changed.

I know I don't have to. I want to. And I want to show you Sand Island. Soon.

In a moment of bravery, Amy responded, Is this from Eric Wilson or his mother?

To which Eric quickly countered: Funny.

And then he pulled out of the driveway, pausing long enough to wave before heading up Vine Street then turning right onto Main. Amy walked back to the house, sat down on the steps then rested her hand on the empty place where the stair rail had been.

"Lord, if You're going to do something, please do it quickly," she whispered. "Because things are getting complicated."

# Chapter Fifteen

Amy blew out a long breath as she hauled the giant stack of files into the file room. Dee was still out sick, which meant Amy not only answered the phone and acted as receptionist, but she also had her own duties to perform.

Thank goodness for Nancy, who knew how difficult Amy found multitasking to be. She'd set up a schedule with Cassie Jo filling in at Dee's chair for one hour in the morning and another hour in the afternoon so that Amy could get things accomplished. The plan meant that some of Cassie Jo's grooming clients had to be rescheduled, but at least the clinic continued to operate without the chaos that might have otherwise ensued.

Amy heard Nancy's office door open. "Aren't you going to stop for lunch?" Nancy called as she stepped into view in the doorway.

"Soon as I'm done with the filing," Amy said as she went back to her task. "I've got the afternoon clients' files pulled, but I hated to leave these out there."

"Working during lunch?" Nancy chuckled. "And I thought dating the doc gave you special privileges."

Stunned, Amy whirled around to face Nancy. "What did you say?"

Nancy's grin went south, and she replaced it with a surprised expression. "I'm sorry, Amy. I just thought that…" She began to turn red. "I didn't mean anything by it."

"I'd expect that kind of teasing from Cassie Jo, but not you, Nancy," she said as her heart drummed a furious rhythm in her chest as she leaned as casually as she could against the filing cabinet.

"I'm only partly teasing, actually." Nancy shifted positions to study her nails before looking back toward Amy. "I'm not suggesting that you're getting any sort of special favors for working here. That's just joking around. Look at you. You work as hard as we do. Harder sometimes. But we all have eyes around here, and we've all seen how he looks at you when you're not aware of it."

Amy swallowed hard then tightened her grip on the file cabinet. Had she a response, she still would have been unlikely to say it. Not with her knees shaking and tears threatening.

She pushed away thoughts of yesterday's almost-date. "Dr. Wilson and I are just friends," Amy said. "And that's all there is to it." *For now, anyway.*

Eric's footsteps echoed in the back office, and Amy inhaled sharply. The last thing she wanted was for him to become involved in this conversation. Nancy must have felt the same for she quickly made her excuses and fled the file room.

"Leaving for lunch, Dr. Wilson?" Amy heard Nancy say.

"I am," he responded. "I need to see a man about a doorbell."

Amy held her breath, praying that Eric wouldn't spy her in the file room and come in to make conversation. The last thing she needed right now was more talk of the two of them going around the office. Especially when things were so very complicated.

She made quick work of her task, and soon she joined Cassie Jo and Nancy in the break room. She paused at the door to be sure she was not being discussed and then stepped inside.

"That was fast," Cassie Jo said as she took a bite of her sandwich.

"I really wanted to get it over with," Amy said as she walked over to retrieve her lunch and drink from the fridge. "And with the case-load this afternoon, I suspect I'll be working late, anyway. No sense in adding to that."

Cassie Jo nodded. "I know you're only here temporarily, but you're such a hard worker. I can't imagine how we'll find someone to take your place when you're gone."

"I doubt you'll have any trouble with that," Amy said. "Besides, you three did fine before I came to work here."

"That was before your story broke and every single woman in a three-state area suddenly needed her dog attended to."

Amy settled in the chair between Nancy and

Cassie Jo. "Technically it wasn't my story, and I'm glad that craziness is over."

"Imagine Dr. Wilson's face when he saw the paper that day." Cassie Jo nudged Amy. "I have to tell you, things were awfully boring around here before you took that call over at the classifieds department. Weren't they, Nancy?"

Nancy nodded then cleared her throat and turned to regard Amy with a concerned expression. "About what I said earlier…"

"It's fine, Nancy," Amy said.

"What's fine?" Cassie Jo looked first at Amy and then at Nancy. "What did I miss?"

"Nothing," Amy said firmly as she gave Nancy a look that she hoped would convey how little she wished to continue this discussion. Burying her nose in the novel she kept in her purse drove home the point.

The remainder of the lunch hour was spent in blessed silence, with Amy engrossed in the novel, Nancy playing a game on her phone and Cassie Jo perusing a fashion magazine. When the back-door alarm chirped, Amy's heart lurched. Eric. He'd returned.

Her gaze flew to the doorway and the hall

beyond, waiting for Eric to walk past. When he did, head down and his attention completely focused on his phone, Amy held her breath. Only when his office door closed did she relax. Then the door opened again and Eric retraced his steps, still not pausing to acknowledge her or anyone else in the break room.

*A hello would have been nice.*

The moment the thought occurred, Amy cringed. This was a job. Eric was her employer. So what if he happened to be a whole lot of fun and a really nice guy? And so what if she could still remember the feeling of running into him and watching him crunch ice cubes in her kitchen?

So he repaired her grandfather's swing. And asked her for a date. Almost.

Work was work. And Eric was right. This was complicated. And so were her feelings.

Shaking off the knowledge that she was acting like a silly schoolgirl, Amy forced her mind back on her work then glanced at the clock. "Time to go back and take Dee's place at the reception desk," she said as casually as she could.

Amy rose to put away her lunch box then tucked the novel into her purse while Nancy set aside her phone. "Ladies, do not start playing that chicken game. I swear it's addictive," Nancy said with a chuckle as she stood and headed for her office.

Cassie Jo tossed the magazine back on the table. "Sometimes I'm glad I don't have the attention span for video games."

Sharing a laugh with Cassie Jo, Amy turned the corner into the hall and almost collided with Eric. Had he not caught her elbows with his hands, she might have gone tumbling backward.

"Oh, I'm sorry" came out in a gasp.

Eric's eyes widened then, quickly, he released his grip on her arms.

Amy took a step backward. "I didn't realize you were standing there."

"What happened, Amy?" Cassie Jo whirled into the hall then stopped short. "Oops. Sorry, boss," she said to Eric. She pressed past both of them then turned to make a funny face at Amy behind Eric's back. Cassie Jo hurried into the back office then peeked around the corner at them. A quick wiggle of her brows told Amy she was up to trouble.

Amy bit her lips and tried not to react. "Did you want something, Dr. Wilson?"

His phone made the sound that she now recognized as an incoming text. He glanced down at it then back at Amy. "Could I speak to you a moment?" Eric looked behind him and almost caught Cassie Jo spying. Or perhaps he did. "In my office, please?"

"Of course," she said as she followed Eric down the hall to his office.

"Cassie Jo," he said as he turned around to see her watching. "Catch the phone while I talk to Amy, would you?"

She had the decency to blush. "Yes, Dr. Wilson."

"And hold off on opening the door unless someone's waiting. This will only take a minute."

"Yes, Dr. Wilson," she said again as she disappeared into the office.

While he claimed the chair behind his desk, Amy settled on the one opposite him. He appeared to be absorbed in whatever the text had said and then in his response. She glanced over his head to the diplomas, both framed in the deep maroon color of his alma mater, Texas A&M University.

Beneath the diplomas was a piece of art in a simple black frame. Three baby pictures, obviously belonging to the Wilson girls, had been framed side by side with a Bible verse running the length of the frame beneath the photographs, it's message written in beautifully done calligraphy: *"Fathers, do not exasperate your children; instead, bring them up in the training and instruction of the Lord." Ephesians 6:4*

Swiveling slightly, Amy spied a painting of an antique sailboat, its sails billowing in the breeze and the sea waves blowing and tossing the craft about. A small silver plaque beneath the painting read It Is Well With My Soul.

"My brother." When she jolted to turn toward him, Eric gestured to the painting. "My brother's an artist. He did that one for my dad."

"It's beautiful," she said softly.

"Beautiful," he echoed as he met her gaze. "Yes, I would agree."

A pause sizzled between then. And then Amy said, "So, you wanted to see me."

"Yes." Pushing the phone aside, Eric leaned back and rested his hands in his lap. "Two things I wanted to talk to you about. First, take a look at this." He reached into his desk drawer and retrieved what looked like a hardware catalog. "The page is marked."

Amy accepted the catalog and turned to the place where he'd put a sticky note. Doorbells. Dozens of them. Except for the color, they all looked pretty much alike.

She looked up at Eric, who had shed his serious expression and was now beaming. "They're…nice," she managed.

Eric laughed. "Any strike you as nicer than the rest?"

Making a valiant attempt to discern the best of the lot, Amy finally gave up and pointed to one in the center of the page. "That one's pretty."

"All right," he said. "I'll let Mr. Kistler down at the hardware store know." He put the catalog away then took another look at his phone before turning his focus on Amy. "So, the other thing. Tomorrow after work. Are you busy?"

Color flooded her cheeks, and she managed a nod. To her surprise, Eric's hopeful expression fell. "So, you're busy?"

"What? No," she hurried to correct. "I'm not busy."

The office intercom buzzed. Frowning, Eric pressed the button. "Yes?"

"Sorry, boss," Nancy said, "but you told me to let you know as soon as the labs came back on the McGill collie."

"Thanks, Nancy. Go ahead and put them on the top of my in-box stack. I'll get to them as soon as I can." He shook his head. "I'm going to have to be quick before we're interrupted again."

Amy laughed. "We do seem to have—"

His phone buzzed, and Eric picked it up and tossed it into the drawer with a flourish. "All right," Eric said as he shut the drawer. "You're not busy tomorrow after work, correct?"

"Correct," she said as she tamed her smile.

"I would really like to take you sailing tomorrow."

"Sailing?" Amy hoped her smile belied her

concern at the seasickness she would have to best before she could step aboard.

"Yes, with my daughters." He seemed to be studying her. "You don't mind that the girls are going with us, do you?"

"Mind?" Amy shook her head. "I love the idea."

And she did. With three little Wilson girls in attendance, perhaps her seasickness wouldn't be as noticeable.

"Good," he said. "We'll have a picnic on Sand Island and be back by sunset."

Apprehension shook her, and Amy made a note to pick up seasickness medication this afternoon on her way home. "That does sound lovely."

It did. As did seeing Sand Island up close for the first time. And with the girls there, anything complicated could be avoided. Surely she could manage it.

"You'll keep it quiet," he said gently. "From the others here, I mean. It could get…"

"Complicated?" Amy offered.

He lifted a dark brow. "Too late for that. How about *more* complicated?"

They shared a laugh then a comfortable

silence fell between them, broken only by the buzzing of Eric's cell phone in the drawer. He slid the drawer open a notch then cringed.

"I should get this one," he told her.

"Yes, of course." Amy rose and scurried from the room. As she walked toward the receptionist desk to take over Dee's afternoon duties, she stifled a grin.

Cassie Jo met her at the desk. "Good news," she said, beaming. "Dee just called. She's no longer contagious so she can come back tomorrow."

"Good!" Amy exclaimed before taking the chair vacated by Cassie Jo. "Did you tell her we missed her?"

"Of course. Oops, that looks like my one o'clock out there." The groomer nodded as she snagged the keys and went to open the door.

After that, the remainder of the day flew by until suddenly it was time to go home. Amy had seen Eric only a few times during the busy afternoon, and mostly from a distance as he and Nancy discussed a patient or studied case files.

Always, however, their gazes met even across the room. And always his steady glance, his slow and secret smile. And always though she tried her best not to react, butterflies danced in her stomach and her lips wanted to turn up in a silly grin.

And as she picked up her seasickness medication on her way home, for the first time since she arrived in Vine Beach Amy had to wonder if her stay here was no longer temporary.

"Lord," she said as she pulled into Nana's driveway, "whatever You're going to do, please hurry."

# Chapter Sixteen

After work on Tuesday, Amy gathered her things and went to her car as casually as she could manage. Inside she was a bundle of nerves, but she made sure no one had seen her with the seasickness pills. And the other ladies in the office certainly were not going to catch her fraternizing with the boss. They'd finally got the message about the teasing, but Amy couldn't miss the looks they exchanged when they thought she didn't see.

So, as planned, she drove home and exchanged her lunch bag for a beach bag then slipped her swimsuit on under shorts and a T-shirt. By the time Amy stepped out onto the porch to wait, Eric was driving up.

Alone.

"Where are your daughters?" she asked as Eric opened the door and helped her inside the truck.

"I'm not exactly sure." One hand on the door, Eric shook his head. "Found a note from Mom saying that she and the girls would be back 'at the usual time.' Whatever that means."

Amy reached for the seat belt and clicked it into place. "That's odd."

"I thought so, too." He swiped at his forehead with the back of his hand. "I called to remind her of our plans, but it went to voice mail. So I thought we'd stop by and see if they've returned."

"All right."

He closed the door and jogged around to climb into the driver's seat. A few minutes later, they were traveling down Main Street.

"So," Eric said as he pulled the truck to a stop at the red light on Main, "I'm curious. Why haven't you been to Sand Island?"

Holding her breath a moment, Amy considered her answer. "This is my first opportunity," she said. The truth, for she'd never considered any other offer before now.

Eric seemed to consider the statement a moment. Then, slowly, he nodded. "Then I suppose it's time."

"Yes," she said, "I suppose it is."

A few more turns and the truck arrived in the driveway of the Wilson home. Eric shifted the truck into Park, frowning. He reached for his phone and made a call then set it aside. "No answer," he said. "Can't imagine why they're not here."

Again he punched in a number. After a minute, he said, "Mom, I had plans to take the girls sailing. Where are you? Call me."

Amy sat very still and tamed her disappointment that the evening was about to end early. When Eric shifted the truck into Reverse, she gave him a sideways look.

"Maybe another time," Amy said.

"Another time?" Eric shook his head. "Let's don't give up yet." He returned the truck to Park and reached for the phone. "I should have thought of this," he said as he typed out a text and then sent it. "I told her to bring the girls directly to the boat. We'll go on and prepare to sail. That way we won't be wasting daylight." He sat the phone down and shifted into Reverse again. "And we can sail soon as the girls arrive."

A few minutes later, they arrived at the docks. "That's her over there," Eric said as he pointed to a pretty white sailboat at the end of the row. Parking the truck, he bounded out and around to open her door for her. "This is going to be fun," he said with a grin.

As she watched the vessel rocking at anchor, Amy climbed and clutched her bag. Maybe she should take another seasickness pill.

"Ready?" Eric asked as he shut the tailgate.

"Ready," she responded with as much enthusiasm as she could muster.

Above the afternoon sky was marked with only a few clouds, and the normally strong wind was but a slow breeze. With hours before sunset yet to go and the midday heat mostly gone, it was the perfect time for a sail.

*I can do this.*

"Follow me," Eric said as he brushed past holding a cooler in one hand and carrying a navy-blue bag over his shoulder.

She said a prayer and stepped onto the dock. Immediately the swaying beneath her feet stopped Amy in her tracks.

And yet, Eric was oblivious.

*Think about something else. Focus on the boats. Ignore the fact they're rocking with the tide.*

Amy took two steps and had to stop. On the horizon she could see Sand Island. *Think of the picnic. Of swimming in the warm Gulf of Mexico. Of having an adventure with Eric and his daughters.*

This brought a smile.

Slowly she inched forward until Amy had almost managed a normal pace. By the time Eric dropped the cooler and bag and then stepped aboard the sailboat, she'd crossed half the distance toward him.

An unexpected gust of wind blew past just as her foot caught on a loose board. Amy stumbled to a halt.

Taking a deep breath, Amy gathered her wits. Then she spied Eric. He'd left the bag and cooler on the dock and was leaning over looking at something. Eric picked up something that appeared to be heavy, such was the motion of his shoulders and the expression on his face. When he moved, Amy saw it was a coil of rope.

Why hadn't she noticed before now how very handsome he was? How suited he was to this life? To this sailboat? What must it have taken for him to consider putting the vessel up for sale?

She watched while he worked, smiling. His tanned arms moved with precise efficiency as he went about what she assumed was his pre-sail routine. A light breeze ruffled the hem of his shirt and caused him to pause and run his hand through his dark hair.

When Eric leaned back onto the dock to retrieve the items he'd left there, he cast a sideways glance in her direction. "Change your mind?" he called.

"No," Amy said with what she hoped would be a casual expression. "Of course not." She clutched her bag and forced a deep breath. "Just admiring the view."

He straightened to look toward Sand Island. "We picked a good day for a sail. So come on and I'll show you around."

Ignoring her ridiculous fears, Amy locked gazes with Eric and moved toward him. Water was water, she decided, whether you were standing in it, swimming in it or sailing in it. And today she was sailing with Eric Wilson.

What could be awful about that?

Eric took her bag then reached to grasp Amy's hand and helped her onto the deck. "Have you sailed before?"

"No," she said as the craft moved under her feet. "Does it show?"

"Maybe a little," he said with the beginnings of a smile. He nodded toward her hands. "Might need to let go of me at some point or we'll never cast off."

Horror struck her at the realization she still held his hands in a death grip. "Oh, I'm sorry," she said as she quickly released him.

"It's fine." His expression was sweet, patient. "It's going to take a minute or two to get your sea legs, so don't be too hard on yourself. Why don't you sit down and just let yourself get used to the feeling of being on the sailboat first?"

She gave Eric a grateful nod then maneuvered her knocking knees toward the spot where he indicated. As Amy sank onto the cushioned surface and grasped the sturdy wooden rail, Eric's phone rang.

He moved to the other side of the boat and faced the ocean, turning his back to Amy. Snatches of words caught on the breeze and drifted toward her, but nothing she could decipher. When he turned around, however, there was no mistaking his mood.

"Apparently my mother forgot the girls had ballet class. She's already taken them and they're in class." He stuffed the phone into his pocket. "Either we sail without them or we reschedule our excursion to Sand Island."

Neither sounded advisable when he said them aloud, and yet both held some measure of appeal. He must have mistaken her hesitation for disappointment, for Eric hastened to say, "Don't worry, we can always pick another afternoon. We've got the whole summer ahead of us." Then he paused. "Or do we?"

Amy shifted positions and found comfort in resting her back against the rail. "What do you mean?"

He moved toward her with the agility of a man obviously comfortable at sea. As he settled beside her, Amy fought the urge to smile in spite of her roiling nerves.

"You did say your stay in Vine Beach was temporary. Given that fact, I just wonder how much time we have to see Sand Island." He paused. "Together, that is."

*Together.*

She inhaled the salt air and let it settle in her lungs while she contemplated a response. Slowly, she exhaled and grinned. "I say let's sail without them."

Eric almost let out a good solid "Whoop" in response to Amy's statement. But the poor woman was already uncomfortable aboard the boat. Why scare her to death, as well?

So he gently nodded, added a grin and then went about the process of setting sail before Amy could change her mind.

As unstable as her footing appeared, he knew he had a few minutes. But if he allowed her to flee she might not come back. Not that she'd indicated she would be in Vine Beach long. She hadn't.

He looked at her from behind the wheel and

caught her staring off toward Sand Island. Allowing himself time to study her while she was occupied with her thoughts, Eric paused his work.

Golden curls hung in wild array over shoulders of nearly the same golden-brown and lifted in the breeze to reveal a slender neck. She wore yellow again today, obviously a favorite color, and this time she'd matched her top with a pair of white shorts and sandals that weren't the best choice for a slick boat deck.

Next time he'd have to educate her on the proper footwear. Maybe take her to get some appropriate shoes.

If there was a next time.

Amy pulled what looked like a green bracelet off her wrist and used it to tie her hair into a ponytail. Still she seemed to be watching the horizon. A gull screeched overhead, distracting both of them. When he looked back at Amy, she was staring at him.

"Do you need some help with anything?" she called.

*Only in keeping my focus off you and on what I should be doing.*

"Thanks, but I'm used to doing this alone."

He gestured to the place beside him. "If you've found your sea legs, you could come join me."

She rose then abruptly landed back on the seat. Thankfully, she seemed to find the humor in her clumsiness and lack of balance.

Eric came to her rescue, and offered her his hand. She accepted his assistance and stood by, holding tight to him. "Don't try to walk yet," he said as he wrapped his arms around Amy's waist to steady her.

And then the closeness of her almost undid him. Eric became acutely aware of the feel of her hand against the bare skin of his arm and the way her hair brushed his shoulder when her ponytail caught the breeze.

He looked down at her and felt the strangest combination of emotions. Like that moment on the porch when he'd been overwhelmed with guilt and happiness all tangled up together, he felt the strong urge to bolt and run. This time, however, Eric knew he would stay.

And hold her until she no longer needed his help to stand.

*Then maybe she can help me stand.*

Continuing to watch her was almost more

than he could manage. And yet he did not want to look away.

"Eric?" She met his stare. "I think I'm ready."

With a nod, he tightened his grip. "All right. Here's how you walk on a moving sailboat."

And then he showed her. Slowly. Gently. Moving her across the deck to the spot he'd saved for her. And with each step his feelings got more complicated. Not that he allowed Amy to see it.

She reached over to grasp the rail, one hand still gripping his, then shook her head. "I feel like a total fool."

"Don't be so hard on yourself," he said. "You're doing great."

Rolling her eyes, Amy laughed. "Hardly. I'm walking like a grandmother and I'm certainly not impressing you."

"You have no idea," he said truthfully. "And as for walking like a grandmother, I can tell you that my own mother, who is a grandmother, usually refuses to sail with me because she cannot manage to do what you're doing."

"Really?" The deck shifted, and she squealed

then turned to grasp him in what would otherwise have appeared to be a tight embrace.

His palm pressed against her back as Amy rested her forehead on his shoulder. "Just stay right here until you're ready to try again."

Eric froze. *Stay right here until you're ready to try again.*

The statement hit him in the gut. Walking across the deck for Amy or risking a broken heart again for Eric, the difficulty factors weren't that different. Both were slow and difficult prospects. But with Amy in his arms, Eric was almost sure he was ready to make the attempt.

"I'm ready to try," Amy said, slicing through Eric's thoughts.

He looked down at the woman in his arms and felt a strange peace. "Then so am I."

And together they crossed the distance to the spot he'd picked out for Amy. Easing her into place, he reluctantly released her.

"You did it," he said. "Good job."

*At least one of us has managed it.*

"I was pathetic." Amy's laughter settled in his heart and brought a smile. "But I'll get the hang of it. I promise."

"Yes, you will." *After you've sailed with me a few more times,* he almost added. "Are you ready to set sail?"

"I am." She looked around then returned her attention to Eric. "What should I do?"

He shook his head. "Normally I have someone cast off while I maneuver things down here but I don't see how—"

"No," she said firmly. "I can do this." She let out a long breath and appeared to be gathering her focus. Or maybe her courage. "All right. What do I need to do?" When Eric told her, she nodded.

"You don't have to do this," Eric hastened to add. "I can manage just fine."

Amy reached to touch his shoulder. "Eric," she said slowly as she stood, bracing herself by holding tight to the rail, "if I don't do this now, I'll never find the courage to try it again. So, if you'll excuse me, I'm going to walk over there and—Oh, no!" A teenager on a water ski zoomed by with a roar, rocking the boat and causing Amy to let go and fall back onto her seat.

"Are you all right?" Eric demanded as he

watched the smart-aleck kid circle around to head east toward the bay.

"Well, that came out of nowhere," she managed as she waited until the wake settled then once again climbed to her feet.

"Yeah, it did," he said. "Probably put in over at the boat ramp on the other side. These kids love to play daredevil on those things. I'm surprised there's just one of them. They usually travel in packs."

"I'm just jumpy. It will be fine." She shrugged and looked toward the horizon where the kid on the water ski was getting smaller as he drove away. "Actually, it looks like fun."

"It is," Eric said. "Though I've only rented them." He shook his head. "Anyway, if you're sure you can handle it, I'll take the wheel and work the sails. We should be at Sand Island in no time."

Her smile wasn't quite as broad as usual, but Amy tackled the task of traversing the length of the sailboat with determination. When she lifted the rope in a gesture of victory, Eric actually cheered for her.

"Come on back and sit beside me," he

called. "It's the best seat in the house and I wouldn't want you to miss the view."

The truth was, he didn't want to miss the view of Amy Spencer enjoying her first sail. And when she managed to return to her spot without a single misstep, Eric congratulated her again, this time with a high five.

Though what he really wanted to do was to kiss her.

He decided the direct route to Sand Island was the best and fastest. Pointing the vessel in the right direction, Eric leaned back to enjoy the ride. A familiar site on these cruises caught his eye, and he nudged Amy.

"Look over there," he said as he pointed to two dolphins crisscrossing their wake just a few yards away.

"Oh, Eric." She swiveled to get a better look at the playful pair. "I've seen them following the ferry across Galveston Bay, but I've never been this close."

"I've seen them come closer, but those two look like they're having too much fun to be curious about us." He glanced over at the island to gauge the distance. "We'll likely have them with us for another ten or fifteen minutes. They'll usually follow the boat until we lay anchor. Guess we're not as interesting sitting still."

The remainder of the cruise, Eric divided his time between tending the needs of the sailboat and watching Amy have a grand time. When the time came to lay anchor, he made sure he got as close as he could manage to the island.

"It's so much smaller than I thought," Amy said as she shielded her eyes from the sun. "And look at the shells. You can see them from here."

"Apparently the island doesn't get much in the way of visitors," he said as he finished preparing the boat. "The girls had their pick of all kinds of shells. I had to play mean Dad and make them leave most of what they had planned to take."

"Awww," she said. "I hope you won't play meanie to me. I just might have to have some of those shells for the glass bowl on my nightstand."

"I suppose I'll let you get away with that," he said. "But for now we need to get to the island." He gave her a mock-critical look. "I hope your swimming abilities are more advanced than your sailing skills."

Amy laughed. "Actually, I've got trophies to prove just how good my swimming abilities are." Steadying herself against the rail, she moved toward the bow where the island was closest. "This looks pretty shallow."

"About ten feet right here, but the slope toward the beach is pretty steep, so you don't have to swim far before you can touch bottom and walk the rest of the way." He gestured to the float where the cooler and bags were now sitting. "Or you can climb aboard with the supplies. There's no shame in it."

Amy gave him a sideways look. "I might have been raised in Houston, but I'm a beach girl at heart. Now," she said as she kicked off her shoes, "I'm of a mind to swim to Sand Island. What about you?"

He grinned but said nothing as he watched her toss her T-shirt and sunglasses aside then step out of her shorts. Her swimsuit was the same color of blue as her eyes. Out this far from land there was little to rock the boat, and yet he felt his knees threatening to bring him to the deck.

She grasped the rail with both hands and leaned over to look down into the water. "Looks like our dolphin friends won't be joining us." Then, slowly, Amy glanced over her shoulder. "All right, Dr. Wilson. Let's go see Sand Island." A pause and then she laughed. "Bet I can beat you there."

Without warning, Amy dived in.

"Hey!" He threw aside his shoes and sunglasses then, without bothering to remove his shirt, dived in. The water was warm, the current nonexistent this far from shore. And yet, by the time his fingers touched sand, he looked up to see Amy standing above him.

"Maybe next time," she said as she shook off the water and sat down beside him.

Eric rolled onto his back and let the waves lap over him as he stared up into the cloudless sky. Life was good.

"Oh, look." Amy leaned into his line of sight and held out a sand dollar. "I used to find those all the time when I was a little girl but I never see them anymore."

Eric sat up and rested his elbows on his knees as he watched Amy gently rinse off the shell. Beyond her, the sailboat he'd once considered selling bobbed at anchor. Life was good. Very good. And he still wanted to kiss her.

# Chapter Seventeen

While Eric swam toward the sailboat to retrieve their dinner, Amy waded out in the warm water. As the waves swirled around her knees and then her waist, she followed Eric's progress.

Once Eric climbed aboard the boat, Amy turned her attention to the shore and the sandy, sparsely populated expanse of Vine Beach. From her vantage point, her grandmother's cottage looked like a dollhouse, the white picket fence small as matchsticks.

A loud splash behind her caused Amy to startle. She whirled around to see a spotted silver fish, a mullet, gliding toward open waters in the company of a half-dozen others. One by one, the fish jumped and splashed as they disappeared from sight.

"Everything all right?" Eric called.

She turned toward the sound of his voice. "I could catch dinner if I had a fishing pole."

Eric laughed. "Want me to grab one?"

"No, I was teasing," Amy said with a chuckle. "I'm sure whatever you've got in the cooler will be wonderful."

He shaded his eyes. "Even if I made it myself?"

"Hmm…might want to grab that fishing gear."

Eric hefted the raft containing the cooler and towels overboard then dived off the sailboat in an easy, graceful arc. He bobbed to the surface, shook the water off his face and aimed the raft toward the beach.

"Race you," he called. "And this time I'll win."

"Deal." Amy dived beneath the surf and, to her horror, collided with something slimy and definitely fish. She screamed and swallowed seawater as the mullet fled.

Touching her toes to the sandy sea bottom, Amy struggled to remain above water. Her foot slipped and she fell hard, banging her head against something sharp.

She sputtered as she fought to regain her balance. Then the horizon tilted.

"Amy, stop," a voice said against her ear. Eric.

She went limp. Somehow the water fell away and she landed on warm sand. Amy opened her eyes to see Eric's face.

"Can you breathe?" he asked.

She nodded. Or at least she thought she could. Fresh air hit her lungs, and Amy began to cough. And cough.

Eric tilted her up to lean against his shoulder. "Amy?"

"I'm fine," she managed. "Now," she added as an afterthought.

He held her at arm's length, his gaze capturing hers. "Are you sure?"

This time Amy knew she'd nodded. Eric smiled.

Then he gathered her into his arms, and she rested her head on his shoulder. "What happened?" he said.

"I feel like a complete idiot. There was this fish and…" Amy shook her head. "I'm a good swimmer. Have been since I was little."

Eric's chuckle rumbled against her ear. "Of course you are," he said gently. "You beat me in our first race."

Leaning away, Amy caught him studying her. "And you've beaten me in the second one."

"Considering we arrived on the beach together, I'd say this one was a tie."

"I suppose…" Her gaze locked with his as her lip began to quiver. "Have I mentioned that I feel like a complete idiot?"

He finger-traced the outline of her mouth. "Oh, Amy," Eric whispered. Softly, gently, with one hand on her back and the other cradling her head, Eric kissed her.

A moment later, he ended the kiss to hold her in his arms. "Things just got complicated, didn't they?" he said against the top of her head.

"Maybe," she whispered. "You might need to kiss me again to be sure."

And so he did. Only when a loud buzzing noise distracted her did Amy break off the kiss. Spying the source, she shook her head. "Stupid water ski," she whispered.

"Hey," the kid called. "You missing a raft?"

"The raft," Eric echoed as he broke off the embrace and scrambled to his feet. "Oh, no."

He bounded across the sand and into the

water. Amy stood despite her shaking knees and watched as Eric chased down the raft that had somehow been forgotten during her episode with the fish.

And the kisses.

Touching her lips, she closed her eyes. "Lord, whatever You're doing," she whispered. "it's getting…" She almost said *complicated.* Instead, she added, "interesting."

Eric came back pushing the raft ahead of him. As he reached the beach, he grasped the rope and hauled the small craft ashore. "Looks like everything's fine. Just a little damp." He gestured to the bag containing their towels. "Guess we'll have to do without a place to sit."

Amy shrugged. "I'm already sandy. I don't mind."

"All right, then." Eric lifted the cooler out of the raft and set it on the sand between them. A few minutes later, he'd spread a feast of fried chicken and all the trimmings out for them to enjoy. "I didn't make this," he confessed. "I'm more of a barbecue man. But with the increase in business at the clinic, I haven't had much time for that." He handed her a plate and gestured to the food. "Help yourself."

The food was wonderful, and so was the company. The awkward moment that followed their kiss had passed, and now conversation flowed. Eric spoke about sailing, about how life after college and veterinary school caused him to give up things like motorcycle racing, and how very much he longed to see his girls grow up with the same small-town life as he had.

Amy listened, studying his every move. She noted that when he smiled, the corners of his eyes crinkled. And when he laughed, those same brown eyes narrowed. She watched him toss bits of food to the gulls, all the while warning her that feeding the birds was the worst sort of thing to do if you wanted them to leave you alone.

But most of all, she watched how he looked at her. How he gave her his full attention when she chattered on about flower arranging and her inability to multitask. How when he was distracted by something, such as a gull that flew too close, his voice would grow soft.

Finally, when the last of the strawberry pie had been consumed, Eric closed up the cooler and placed it in the raft. The sun danced orange and gold across the waves and threatened to soon dip beneath the horizon.

A glance at the beach told her they were among the few still enjoying the remains of the day. Across Vine Street, the lights were coming on in the houses, most notably the King place next door to Nana's cottage. The modest King home was lit like a beacon, with lamps on in every room and a porch light blazing.

"We should go," Eric said as he returned to recline beside her, belying his intention to actually make good on the statement with any sort of haste.

Amy nodded. "Probably, but the sunset is just so pretty."

Eric rolled onto his side and supported his head with his palm, and Amy did the same. "And so are you."

She smiled. "I don't know what to say to that."

He reached to push away a strand of her hair from her face. "Don't say anything. Just let me kiss you one more time before we leave."

And so she did.

"Amy," he said softly after the kiss ended,

"you should know that I didn't bring you to Sand Island for this. It was just going to be a trip to the island with you and the girls." He paused as their gazes collided. "I never planned to kiss you."

"Sorry you did?" she dared ask.

"No" was his quick response. "Not at all."

"I'm not sorry, either." She looked past Eric to the gray waters of the Gulf. "But this makes things even more…" Amy struggled to find another word besides *complicated*. "Difficult," she finally said as she returned her attention to the veterinarian. "For both of us, I'm sure."

He sat up and dusted the sand off his hands then rested his elbows on his knees. The wind tossed his hair while the setting sun turned his dark hair a golden-brown.

"Difficult." Eric said the word as if turning it over in his mind. "Actually, kissing you was easy. I didn't think about it. And it felt right."

"It did," she agreed.

His smile was broad. "Glad we got that worked out. Now, much as I would enjoy sitting here awhile longer, we need to get back to port before it gets too dark."

Reluctantly, she allowed Eric to help her to her feet. Their swim back to the sailboat was slow, leisurely, and when Amy climbed aboard then took the contents of the raft from Eric, she felt a tiny surge of regret that the afternoon was almost over.

By the time they'd docked and loaded the truck, regret had become anticipation. Would Eric kiss her again when he took her home?

"So," Eric said as he helped Amy off the boat, "did you have a good time?"

"I did." She reached for the bag but Eric grabbed it first. "Thanks to you, I now know what Sand Island looks like from a vantage point other than my upstairs window."

"Glad I could be of assistance." He shouldered the two bags then picked up the cooler. "After you," Eric said as he gestured toward the parking lot with his free hand.

When they arrived at the truck, Eric opened the door for Amy then tossed the cooler and bags into the back and slammed the tailgate. From where he stood, he could see Amy looking at her phone. A reminder that he hadn't checked his since they returned to the boat after the picnic.

He reached into his bag and hauled out the phone from its waterproof case. One missed call from a number he did not recognize. They had, however, left a message, so he clicked on the icon and listened while the voice mail activated. While he waited, Eric walked around to climb into the driver's seat and shut the door.

"Had a message," he told Amy. "Guess I didn't hear the phone ring while we were on our way back from Sand Island. I need to listen to it in case I've got an emergency with a patient."

"Yes, of course," she said as she switched off her phone and fitted it into her pocket.

"It'll just be a—"

The caller began to speak, and instantly Eric recognized it to be Christy's mom as she said, "Dean and I can't wait to see the girls tomorrow night."

Tomorrow night. Dinner with Christy's parents. It had been planned for months.

His heart sank.

"Something wrong?" Amy asked as he hung up.

Through the swirl of emotions, Eric managed to shake his head. "Just an appointment I'd forgotten about." He noticed what appeared to be a troubled look. "Something wrong?"

"Just an email I hadn't expected."

"Not bad news, I hope." Eric said as he buckled his seat belt.

"A job offer, actually." She slid him a sideways look as he started the truck. "In San Antonio."

"Oh." Disappointment and relief hit him in equal portions. "What are you going to do?"

Amy put the phone away, her attention focused elsewhere. "I don't know."

Thankfully, the distance to Amy's front door was a short one. Before he had time to form a decent excuse for his silence, they'd arrived.

"I'll get your bag," Eric said as he bounded from the suddenly claustrophobic confines of the truck. He carried the bag around the edge of the fence and up the walk to the front door.

Amy pressed past him to unlock the door then dropped the bag inside.

An hour ago he would have taken the opportunity for another of her sweet kisses. In fact, he had. But now, with the sound of Christy's mother still in his ears and news of a job for Amy in San Antonio still stinging, he felt like a fool.

She met his stare, her fingers drumming a rhythm on the door frame. "Would you like to come in?"

"Thanks, but I should get home before the girls go to bed." Eric shoved his hands into his pockets. "To tell them good-night and all."

"Right," Amy said. "Of course." She stepped toward him to offer a hug, and he wrapped her in his arms. Her hair smelled of sunshine and salt air, and her skin still felt warm from the afternoon outdoors.

Eric traced the length of her spine with his palm, resting his hand on the nape of her neck. Even though his gut told him to run, Eric stayed put.

Finally, Amy broke the embrace to look up into his eyes. "Thank you for a wonderful evening, Eric."

*Another kiss. Just one.*

But he couldn't. Wouldn't. So he made his excuses and fled like the fool he was. When he walked in the back door at home, all three girls raced to meet him with his mother trailing behind.

"I'm awfully sorry about the mix-up," his mother said, her face a mask of innocence.

"What mix-up?" Ella asked as she wrapped her arms around Eric's neck.

"Never mind." Mom gave him a look that told him she hadn't mentioned to the girls what they'd missed. "Why don't you tell your dad about dance class, girls?"

As the trio chattered on, Eric tried to listen. But his mind wandered to the battle waging in his heart. As great as this evening had been, and as amazing as the kisses they'd shared had felt, his good mood had been easily ruined by the guilt he felt at hearing his former mother-in-law's voice while Amy sat beside him. Then there was the thought that maybe the Lord was moving Amy away from Vine Beach to whatever awaited her permanently.

"All right, girls," his mother said, "tell your

dad good-night." When they protested, she shook her head. "Enough of that. Daddy needs to get cleaned up and the four of us have an appointment with chapter twelve."

"Chapter twelve?" Eric asked.

"Of the book Grammy's reading to us," Brooke said.

Why didn't he know this? Eric nodded woodenly then embraced each of his daughters before sending them off to follow their grandmother.

Going through the motions, Eric showered and changed into sweatpants and a T-shirt then padded back into the kitchen for a glass of water. He found Mom sitting at the table obviously waiting for him to return.

"What really happened this evening, Mom?" Eric said when he turned to face her. "You knew I was going to take the girls—"

"Hush, Eric," she said in a loud whisper. "They might hear you."

He let out a long breath. "I know what you were doing."

Mom lifted one brow. "Did it work?"

"Mother, you are…" He shook his head.

"Yeah, it worked," he said as he joined her at the table. "But…"

"But?" She leaned over to touch his sleeve. "But you've got second thoughts? About what? Amy?"

"No, she's great." He decided not to elaborate though the expression on his mother's face told him she'd like to know more. "But I'm just not sure the timing's right."

"You're not sure?" his mother echoed. "Eric, really. I've seen how you look at her and, well, believe me, son. You're ready."

"Mom, keep your voice down."

She appeared duly chastised. "All right, but I still don't agree."

"A few hours ago, I wouldn't have, either." He paused to run his hand through his still-damp hair. "Then, while Amy was sitting next to me in the truck, I checked my voice mails. There was a number, and, well, I figured it was a patient with an after-hours emergency." Another pause. "It was Christy's mother."

The air went out of his mother's sails. "I see."

"Yeah. And here I was sitting by the woman I'd just kissed and listening to a reminder of a dinner tomorrow night with my former in-laws."

To his surprise, his mother smiled.

"What? There's nothing amusing about this. I felt awful." He shook his head as he lowered his voice. "Like I was cheating on Christy."

"You kissed Amy?"

"Mom, seriously. Focus." He waited for her to get a grip. When her expression went neutral, Eric continued. "If I were ready, I would never have felt like I did. It was like the whole evening at Sand Island had been some awful…" He stopped to collect his thoughts.

"It felt like you were cheating on Christy," his mother said gently.

"Yeah" came out on a long breath. "It did."

"And Amy isn't like Christy, is she?"

Eric thought of his elegantly well-behaved late wife, of her serious nature and the drive and ambition that she channeled into raising the girls after she left her career in advertising. Of the way every moment of her life was scheduled, every calorie counted, every closet neat and organized. Then he thought about the coconut cake that Amy had eaten two generous slices of. Of how she danced in the sprinkler and had two books going at any given time. Likely if he dared look into a closet, he'd find chaos.

"Amy's kind, and thoughtful. She's good with the girls." Eric scrubbed his face with his palms. "But no, mostly she's very different from Christy."

Chuckling, Mom's eyebrows rose. "And everything in her life is temporary, including her stay in Vine Beach." His mother shrugged. "But I think she's wrong."

"Maybe," he said slowly as he thought of the afternoon he'd just spent with Amy. Of their kisses. "But what I haven't told you is that she got an email while we were sailing. She's got a job offer in San Antonio."

"I see," she said slowly. "Will she be taking this job?"

"She didn't say, but it doesn't matter. I just can't get past the fact that she's so different from Christy. Our marriage was good, you know?" He let out a long breath. "So if it worked with Christy, how can I expect it to work with Amy?"

"Because the two are so different, you mean?"

Eric nodded. "And I won't risk exposing the girls to a failed relationship. Or, worse, to a failed marriage. I just won't."

"And yet you have feelings for Amy."

A statement, not a question. Thus, Eric felt no compunction to respond. And yet, had he been forced to admit the truth, he knew he did.

To allow those feelings to continue would mean putting his heart and his family at risk. And no matter how much he enjoyed spending time with Amy Spencer, he just couldn't take that risk.

The only solution was to stop the madness before it went any further.

His mother reached across the table to cover his hands with hers. "Eric, I want you to listen to me. Will you promise me you'll do that?"

"Yeah, of course, Mom."

"I mean really listen." When he nodded, she continued. "I can't fix this for you. If I could've I would have done it a long time ago. But I can give you some advice that I wish someone had given me." She withdrew her hands to settle them in her lap. "Stop living in the past or you'll have no future."

The same thing Riley Burkett told the group just about every Saturday morning. "Yeah, well, I've heard that before," he told his mother. "But saying it's one thing, and doing it's another."

"Then just do it."

"Just like that, Mother?" he demanded. "You've never had to make this kind of choice."

His mother rose and pressed past him to reach for her purse. "That's where you're wrong, son," she said when she reached the door. "The Lord has plans," she said, "but if you're back where you've been, you'll never see where He wants you to go."

Another saying of Riley's. "You must be eavesdropping on the Starting Over meetings, Mom. Riley says both those things word-for-word almost every week."

She walked to the door as if she hadn't heard. Then, with one hand on the doorknob, his mother turned around to face him. "Where do you think he first heard them?"

And then, with a wink, she was gone.

# Chapter Eighteen

Amy turned off her computer then dialed her grandmother's number three times before she finally got the nerve to press the send button. Nana picked up on the third ring, the sound of the television blaring in the background.

"Amy, hon," Nana said, "let me shut off this noise before I try talking to you." A moment later, she returned to the phone with nothing but silence accompanying her. "Now, what was it you were saying?"

"I was telling you how I went to Sand Island today."

"Sand Island?" Nana's laughter made Amy smile. "Goodness, girl, you've been talking about that place since you were knee-high.

What in the world made you finally decide to see it for yourself?"

"It was a who, actually," she said slowly as she reached for a teacup and set it on the counter. "Eric took me for a sail after work."

"Did he, now?" Nana paused. "And what of this aversion you have to boats, sweetheart?"

"It's not an aversion. It's seasickness. But I handled it." Amy moved into the kitchen. "The seasickness medication worked fine, and we had a wonderful sail. Better than wonderful, actually."

"But?"

Amy filled the teakettle then put it on the stove to boil. "What do you mean, 'but'?"

"But I hear hesitation in your voice," her grandmother said. "What aren't you telling me?"

"Oh, Nana," Amy said as she turned her back on the stove. "I think I'm falling in love with Eric."

Nana giggled. "Honey, you say that like it's a problem. Doesn't he share your feelings?"

"I think so. Or at least I hope so." She sighed as she reached for the tea bags and dropped one in the cup. "Remember how you told me that the Lord would let me know when it was time to leave Vine Beach?" The teapot began to whistle, and Amy turned off the burner then poured the water over the tea bag. "I've thought from the beginning that the answer would come in the form of a job offer. What I mean is, if I had work here, I'd be staying, but if I found a job somewhere else, then I'd be going. So I sent out fifteen résumés, remember?"

"I do, and I suppose that makes sense," Nana said. "Though if you've got feelings for Susan's boy then I don't see what could possibly make you confused about whether you should stay or go."

"I also got a job offer." She stirred a spoonful of sugar into her tea. "A really good one. In San Antonio."

Silence.

"Nana? Did you hear me? I heard back from the owner of the Continental Shop. That's the one that's in the lobby of the Riverwalk Hotel. He sent an email this afternoon saying he needs a manager with design experience, and he's offered me twice what I make here in Vine Beach."

"That's exciting, Amy," Nana said this without much enthusiasm. "It appears you've got a decision to make."

She blew across the surface of the steaming tea then took a sip. "Is it awful that if I knew Eric loved me, I'd gladly give up the job to stay here?"

"Oh, honey," Nana said, "that's not awful at all. In fact, I'd go so far as to recommend that you find out how this young man feels as soon as possible."

"But what if I'm moving too quickly?"

"Well, Amy," her grandmother said, "how soon does the fellow in San Antonio need an answer from you?"

"His email said he would like to schedule a video conference for this week to go over the particulars of the job. Then I would travel to San Antonio to see the store and get acquainted with the staff. He wasn't clear on exactly when he wanted that to happen, but I got the impression he's in a hurry to delegate the work he's now doing himself."

"So you do have a reason to move quickly."

Amy sighed. "Yes, I suppose I do."

"You'll either have to tell this boy how you

feel or plan to keep it to yourself indefinitely. Eric's not likely to pick up and follow you to San Antonio when he's only just got his practice established here."

"I know, Nana." She took another sip of tea and changed the subject to gardening. That sent her grandmother off on a conversation about roses that gave Amy the diversion she sought. Twenty minutes later, she hung up knowing what she needed to do.

By the time she climbed into bed, Amy had her plans set. She would kidnap Eric after work and make a fabulous meal for him. Maybe she'd even suggest they eat in the dining room rather than the porch this time.

Pulling her laptop into bed with her, Amy dug around for the perfect menu. Finally, somewhere in the wee hours of the morning, she'd made her decisions and printed off the recipes. She fell asleep knowing that tomorrow would be quite a day.

When she awoke, the alarm had not yet gone off. Amy rolled over to move the curtains aside and watch the sun rise over Sand Island. Finally she dressed and left for the clinic, anticipation tugging at her as she parked next to Eric's truck.

There was no one in the back office, so she walked down the hall and found Cassie Jo in the break room. "Where is everyone?"

"Dee's not here yet. Nancy and the doc are in surgery. Emergency early this morning. The owner's waiting out front."

"Oh, I didn't look in the waiting room," Amy said as she reached into her purse and pulled out the invitation to dinner she'd composed. While her plan had been to hand it to Eric, perhaps letting him find it was a better idea.

She made her excuses to Cassie Jo and then went in to deposit the invitation on Eric's desk. Her mission accomplished, Amy returned to the office only to find Dee now at the receptionist desk. "Welcome back," she told her. "Feeling better?"

Dee turned around, concern on her face. "Amy, there's a letter on your desk. You might want to read it right now."

"A letter?" She shrugged. "All right. Let me put my purse away first."

"No." Dee cringed. "What I mean is, just read it, all right?"

"All right." Amy sat her purse on the desk and reached for the envelope. She recognized Eric's handwriting immediately.

Inside was a single piece of folded paper and a check written for an amount equal to two weeks salary. Amy set the check aside and opened the letter.

Dear Amy,
I hope you will accept the check as sever-ance pay and understand that I will give you an excellent recommendation and a letter of reference to your employer in San Antonio.

He had signed it Eric T. Wilson, DVM.

Numb, she folded the page and returned it and the check to the envelope. When she looked up, Dee's image was swimming through the tears. "I think I've been fired," Amy said.

Dee rose to hurry to her. "No, honey, you weren't fired. Dr. Wilson made a point of tell-ing us that wasn't the case."

"He told you…" Amy shook her head. "You knew?"

"We all did." Dee leaned close. "We all got a text last night telling us to arrive fifteen minutes early this morning for the staff meeting. He wanted us to be sure and understand that things had changed and you would no longer be working here. He said it like it was a good thing. Something about a job offer elsewhere."

Amy's attention caught on that last statement and held to it, even as she shouldered her purse and walked toward his office. She would correct Eric on that once she saw him. For if he would only ask, Amy knew she would stay in Vine Beach.

"I'm going to leave him a note on his desk," she said over her shoulder. "Would one of you mind letting him know?"

A chorus of yesses followed her as she walked into Eric's office and pulled a slip of paper from the printer behind his desk. In as few words as she could manage she let him know she still wanted to see him this evening. That he'd still be welcome for dinner at the same time, no hard feelings.

Quickly Amy signed her name then folded

the page in half and wrote Eric's name across the paper. Spying a stapler, she sealed the note as best she could then made a fast exit without stopping to chat with her former coworkers.

On her way home, she considered going to visit Nana but decided against it. Instead, Amy took her grocery list into the store and came out a half hour later with the ingredients for what she knew would be a memorable dinner.

By midmorning, she'd begun to worry about Eric's silence. Surely by now he'd seen the dinner invitation. Pacifying her fears with the reminder that Eric's day had started with an emergency surgery, Amy told herself that his schedule was likely thrown off and he was working hard to catch up.

Then came the lunch hour, and she knew he'd somehow manage to call. When he did not, Amy decided to brave a call to him. His voice mail picked up on the second ring, giving Amy cause to believe that Eric was on the other line. Possibly calling her right then. Or speaking to a client. Or his daughters. Didn't he usually go home for lunch with them?

She left a message asking him to call. It

wasn't until sometime after one in the afternoon that Amy began to consider the fact that
Eric might not call her back. Even then, she
decided that maybe he just didn't see the note.
Nancy could have accidentally set files on it
or Dee could have picked it up by mistake
thinking it belonged elsewhere.

Anything could have happened. So Amy
called the office, praying Dee would answer.
"I wonder," Amy said when she heard the familiar voice, "if you could check and see if
Dr. Wilson got something." How to explain
what to look for? "It's an invitation" was all
she decided needed to be said.

"He didn't mention anything about it, and
I haven't been in his office so I couldn't say.
Do you want me to ask him?" Dee asked.

Amy frowned. This wasn't sounding like
she'd hoped. "If you don't mind."

"Of course," Dee said, "but we're kind of
busy because we're closing in an hour. So I'll
grab him when I can and ask. I assume you'd
like me to be discreet."

"Yes, please," Amy said. "And thank you."
She was about to hang up when she thought of
something else. "Dee, would you mind asking

Dr. Wilson to give me a call? Just to let me know he received it."

"So he should call instead of me?" She sounded perplexed.

"If possible" was the best answer Amy could think of. "But if he's busy, well…"

"Right, okay," Dee said. "Sorry but the other line's ringing. Got to go."

Amy hung up the phone and tried not to cry. Something was wrong. Something worse than no longer working at the clinic. And the more time that slipped by, the more she became certain that the problem might be bigger than a complication.

Surely he didn't think she would accept the job without talking to him first. Not after the kisses.

So Amy held on to high hopes as she trudged into the kitchen and began preparing dinner. The last thing she wanted was for Eric to show up and the food not be ready. Thus, she began with the bread dough, kneading as she'd done for so many years at Nana's side. A knock at the door stilled her hands. Was he here already? And without calling?

Wiping flour off as she walked toward the

door, Amy gave passing thought to how she might look.

Pausing at the mirror, Amy dusted flour from her cheek then pasted on a smile and then opened the door. "Eric, I'm so glad…" Her gaze landed on a stranger wearing a name tag that proclaimed his name to be Bob and his employer to be Lumber Guys. "May I help you?"

He offered up a box then gestured to the door frame. "I'm here to install the doorbell."

"You are?" Amy shook her head. "I had no idea that…"

Bob shrugged. "Got the call this morning. Boss said it was a rush job. So," he said as he once again pointed to the door frame, "where do you want it?"

"Anywhere's fine," she said as her hopes deflated slightly.

If Eric was now paying someone to install the doorbell, how likely was it that he would be coming for dinner? "You don't do stair rails, too, do you?"

Bob looked up from his work. "Nah," he said with a shrug. "Not today, anyway. I'll be back on Saturday to get that done. Wood won't be here before then else I'd have added that to today's list."

"I see," she somehow managed before slipping back inside.

A check of her phone revealed there had been no calls. When she adjusted the volume and made sure the battery was charged, Amy tucked it into her pocket and went to see to the dinner that no longer held any appeal.

When there was nothing left to hold her in the kitchen, Amy wandered back onto the porch with her book while the repairman finished his work.

"All done," he said a short time later. "Want to give it a try?"

Amy set aside the book she hadn't read a word of. "No, you go ahead."

Several jabs and rings later, Bob pronounced the doorbell installation complete. He drove away with a promise to return on Saturday after the wood delivery, leaving Amy alone with the phone that refused to ring.

Finally, when she could no longer stand the silence, Amy headed for the beach where her tears would be shed without danger of Eric surprising her. She walked knee-deep in the surf until the marina beckoned up ahead.

Telling herself that she would just stray to within eyesight of Eric's sailboat to check and see if it was docked, Amy dried her eyes and moved that way. When she spied the craft, she continued toward it until she found the walkway.

There Amy paused just long enough to look behind her at the parking lot where she quickly discovered Eric's truck was not among the vehicles parked there. She made her way toward the sailboat, telling herself she was just going to take a peek at it.

Of course, once she stood within reach of the deck, a peek wasn't enough. Slowly, she reached over to climb aboard.

# Chapter Nineteen

Gaido's had always been a favorite place to dine with Christy's parents, even before Christy's illness. When the Tuckers came down for their yearly week at the beach, the first place they came was the seafood restaurant on the Seawall. After the babies started arriving, Eric and Christy began to join her parents in their vacation at the rented beach house.

And then Christy died, and there was no beach vacation that year. The past three years, he'd sent his daughters off alone to enjoy their grandparents. This year would be no different.

Only this year they'd insisted on reviving the Gaido's tradition. Thus, Eric pulled the truck to a stop in the parking lot and stared up at the giant red crab over the entrance.

Taking a deep breath, he made a feeble attempt at preparing himself for the evening ahead. His phone buzzed. A text from the office. Eric sighed. Likely Dee sending him tomorrow's schedule.

Eric stuffed the phone back into his pocket and forced a smile then checked his watch. Half past four. Right on time for the early dinner that had become their tradition. "All right, girls," he said. "Best behavior tonight, okay?"

"Always, Daddy," Hailey said.

"Restaurant voices," he said as he shut off the engine. "And no one talks with her mouth full of food. Got it?"

"Da-a-a-addy," Ella said. "We know how to behave in Gaido's."

"Yeah, Daddy," Hailey said. "It's not like we've never been here before."

"There they are," Brooke squealed. "Come on!"

Eric looked up to see his former in-laws entering the restaurant. "All right," he said on a long breath, "but I miss you girls already."

Brooke slid over the seat to land in his lap.

"Don't be silly, Daddy. We're only going to be gone for a week."

He embraced Brooke. "But what will I do with a quiet house that stays clean all week?"

"Maybe you could call Aaamy," Hailey singsonged from her place behind him.

"Yeah, Daddy," Ella said as she popped over to settle in the passenger seat. "You should take Amy out on a date."

"We like Amy," Brooke said. "She's nice."

"You should have brought her tonight," Hailey said. "Mimi and Grandpa would like her."

Eric gave that thought only a moment's consideration before he discarded it. His decision to follow his conscience and ignore his heart was difficult enough without his daughters making attempts to derail his plans.

Besides, ever since the call came in from the fellow in San Antonio checking Amy's references, he'd taken that as a sign that their time together was at an end. Hadn't she told him more than once that she felt she was only in Vine Beach temporarily?

He allowed the girls to continue their teasing for a moment longer. "All right," Eric finally said. "Enough of that. Let's go in before

Mimi and Grandpa wonder whether we're coming at all. And no discussion about Amy, understand?"

Perhaps while they were gone, he would figure out the best way to tell them about Amy's departure. But not tonight. Not when they'd be gone for a full week.

Eric needn't have worried about the girls saying anything about Amy, for their grandmother brought her up almost before he could place his drink order. "Interesting article about you and the girls in the *Chronicle*," she said as she peered over her menu. "Took us both by surprise."

Eric's heart sank. Of course the Tuckers would have seen the headline.

"Yes," he said as he took a sip of water, "your granddaughters seem to think I need help in an area that I am just fine in."

"Is that so?" Dean Tucker asked the girls. "Maybe Mimi and I should hear your side of the story."

Not even Eric's scathing look could keep his daughters silent as they gleefully answered all their grandfather's questions about the article and their reasons for calling the *Vine Beach Gazette.*

Thankfully, Amy's name did not come up once. When the waiter arrived to take their food order, Eric gave thanks for the distraction. Then Dean began to quiz the girls about their new school and other such topics, and Eric finally breathed a sigh of relief.

By the time the pecan-ball dessert had been devoured and the check had been paid, Eric decided he would escape the evening unscathed. While Alice Tucker took the girls to the ladies' room, Eric walked with Dean to the truck to get their bags.

"Are you sure you won't come along?" Dean asked as he fell into step beside Eric.

"I can't." Eric pulled the truck keys from his pocket. "What with the new practice and all, I can't justify spending so much time away."

"I see." His former father-in-law stopped in front of the truck and placed his hand on Eric's shoulder. "If I ask you a question, will you give me an honest answer?"

"Of course." Eric looked the older man in the eye. "If I can, that is."

"Is there a woman in your life?"

"Other than the girls and my mom?" he joked as he looked beyond Christy's father to the Seawall and the murky gray waters of the Gulf of Mexico.

Dean tightened his grip on Eric's shoulder. "We worry about you," he said. "Christy wouldn't have wanted you to be alone. I think you know that."

"I don't know anything of the sort." Eric shook his head. "Look, I'm sorry, Dean. I appreciate what you're trying to say but…" He sighed and looked away, unable to finish the thought, much less the statement.

"Does she like our girls?"

Eric looked up sharply. "Who?"

He gave Eric an even look. "The woman you're afraid to tell me about."

"I'm not afraid, I—" Eric shook his head. "That's not true. I'm terrified."

A car rolled past then pulled into a space across from them. Eric used the distraction to pull together his thoughts.

"I loved your daughter more than life itself," he finally said, "and I couldn't imagine I'd ever want any woman but her."

"Until…"

"Until I met Amy." There, it was out. "And yes, she likes our girls very much. And they like her. Very much."

Dean laughed. "That's wonderful, Eric. When can we meet her?"

"No, it's not so wonderful, Dean, and I don't expect you'll meet her." He shrugged. "She's leaving Vine Beach to take a job in San Antonio. I made things easy for her and cut off contact today."

"Easy for her?" Dean shook his head. "Sorry, Eric, but it sounds like you chickened out."

He was about to disagree. Then, reluctantly, Eric owned up to it. "Yeah. I guess so."

His former father-in-law leaned against the truck's hood and crossed his arms over his chest. "Why?"

"Guilt, I guess." He spied Alice and the girls just inside Gaido's front door. "I felt like I was cheating on Christy."

"All the time?" Dean asked. "Or just when you allowed the fear to intrude?" He paused long enough to make Eric uncomfortable. "That's what I thought. Now, I won't be telling you what to do." He glanced over his shoulder to wave at Alice, who was herding the girls past the restaurant's brightly lit gift shop and out the door. "But I don't think you're quite at the end of whatever you had with this young lady."

"Daddy!" Brooke called. "Look what Mimi bought for us."

Eric waved to Brooke then returned his attention to Dean. "Why do you say that?"

"If you were, you wouldn't have mentioned it at all, would you? Now, what say we take these little girls off your hands for a week so you can figure out what to do?"

"Dean," Eric said as he gestured for his former father-in-law to follow him to the back of the truck. "She's nothing like Christy. How can God possibly want me to be with someone so different from the woman who made me so happy?"

The older man thought for only a second. "Think, Eric. Can you imagine your life without Amy in it? When you know the answer, then you'll know what to do."

Eric pondered Dean's question all the way back to Vine Beach. When he reached his street, however, he found himself unwilling to go back to an empty house. So he turned right instead of left and headed for the dock.

Maybe he'd find a quiet place and sit for a while. To think. Or maybe not to think at all.

He pulled into the parking lot at a few minutes before seven and sat in air-conditioned silence until the clock on the dash showed exactly seven. Given the fact the sun wouldn't set for an hour or more, a sail wasn't out of the question. Given the amount of driving and thinking he'd done, however, Eric knew he was far too tired to attempt it.

Slamming the truck door, he stuffed his keys into his pocket and headed for the sailboat. Maybe he would sleep out there tonight. The breeze was nice, and according to the weather report he'd heard on the way back, no rain or high winds were predicted.

If he wasn't concerned about being called out on an emergency, Eric might have taken the boat out toward Sand Island and anchored there for the night. But the doctor who was taking calls for him this afternoon went off duty at ten, which left precious little time for any sort of relaxation away from shore.

So Eric headed toward the boat with the

idea of finding a little peace and quiet. And keeping his phone on vibrate until eight with no intention of answering the phone unless Alice or Dean or the girls called.

Or maybe Amy.

He checked his messages one last time and spied a missed call. From Amy. Quickly he dialed the number for voice mail.

"Eric, please call me," Amy's message said. "I wonder if you got the invitation. And what your response is."

He had no idea what invitation she was talking about. Once he decided what to do about their relationship, he'd ask her what she was talking about.

She knew by now that he'd cleared the way for her to take the job in San Antonio, and that he'd arranged to have the doorbell repaired so as to keep him away from her if that helped her to decide. What she might not know is that he had also hired a professional to repair the stair rail. This he'd done because he planned to leave the day open to go to Galveston and spend the weekend with the Tuckers and the girls.

Maybe.

Or maybe not.

He hadn't decided.

Another thing to consider once he got aboard and found the peace and quiet that the sailboat offered.

Walking across the deck of the sailboat was much easier now that she'd done it a few times. Still, when Amy heard the vehicle pull up, she panicked and stumbled. Landing hard on her knee, she covered her mouth to keep from crying out.

A glance down and she knew she'd skinned her knee. At least she'd not done worse, Amy reminded herself as she climbed to her feet and went in search of something to stop the bleeding.

Finding the door to the cabin below locked, Amy had to settle for a discarded sweatshirt she found hanging from the captain's wheel. It was maroon and unlikely to show the damage she was inflicting on it, though Amy knew she would somehow have to bring it home, wash it and return the clean shirt undetected.

Amy sank onto the cushions where such a short time ago she'd sat next to Eric as he sailed toward Sand Island. As she held the shirt to her knee, she felt tears once again threaten.

Worse, so did her seasickness. She leaned her head against the rail and closed her eyes.

"Amy?" Opening her eyes, Amy saw Eric standing in front of her. "What are you doing here?"

"I, well…" She blinked hard to tame her emotions. "I'm not sure, really. I went for a walk and here I am."

"Yes, here you are." His expression was something between confused and angry, or at least that's what Amy could see through the swimming image her tears caused. "I got your message."

"Oh?" Amy said with what she hoped was a casual tone.

"I'm sorry but I have no idea what invitation you're talking about." He glanced down at the shirt covering her knee. "Hey, isn't that mine?"

"It is," she said. "I borrowed it. I'll see that the blood is cleaned off before I return it."

"Blood?" Eric came to sit beside her, lifting the edge of the sweatshirt to spy the mess she'd made of her knee. "Amy, how did you do that?"

"I fell." She shrugged. "I feel really stupid, actually. I shouldn't have come here."

"No, you shouldn't have," he said. "You're trespassing, you know." His serious expression only lasted a moment. "But I'm glad you're here all the same. So, what's this about an invitation?"

"Oh, that." Again Amy tried to appear as if things were not of any great consequence. All the while the butterflies in her stomach were quickly turning to something less sweet. "I left an invitation in your office."

"I didn't see it." He paused. "But now that I think of it, I can't recall going into my office at all other than first thing this morning. We had a busy morning and I left right after lunch to go take the girls to spend a week with their grandparents." He paused to scrub at his face. "Sorry. Long day. What was it the invitation was for again?"

Amy drew in a long breath and let it out slowly. Her stomach turned, her knee hurt and her pride was injured. But most of all, she wished she hadn't come here at all.

"I was going to make dinner for you tonight. I thought it might be nice to…"

"To tell me in person that you were going to take the San Antonio job?"

His tone surprised her. "No, actually I was going to tell you…" She thought better of completing the statement and said, instead, "Never mind. It's probably just as well that you didn't get the invitation."

"Come with me." Eric reached to help her stand then pulled out his key to open the door to the cabin. "I've got a first-aid kit down here."

She complied, and found herself sitting on a padded bench in a tiny kitchen area. "I'm sure it's nothing," she said as she once again dabbed the shirt on the injury.

"Probably not, but I'll fix you up all the same, all right?" Eric reached to remove the sweatshirt from her hand then tossed it aside to retrieve a first-aid kit. "Don't move."

He turned on a lamp and pointed it at her knee. At his touch, Amy closed her eyes, her stomach rolling with the gentle movement of the boat.

"This might sting a little," Eric said. It did,

but she kept her silence even as tears welled in her eyes.

A few minutes later, he had cleaned the wound. While the peroxide burned like fire, it was nothing compared to the seasickness welling up inside. "I should go," she said when he paused to reach for a bandage. "I'm fine, really. Just need to get home."

Eric looked up from his work, one dark brow lifted. "Let me finish this and then I'll take you home."

A statement, not a question. Amy prayed her gut would hold up.

Eric went back to his work and in a few minutes, he had her knee bandaged. "Here, let me help you stand. I want to be sure I haven't taped you too tight."

She managed to get upright but then promptly swayed and landed back on the bench. "I'm sorry," she managed through gritted teeth. "Seasick."

"Need fresh air?" he asked as he reached to pull her back to a standing position.

"Yes, and dry land," she managed. "And quickly."

Eric snagged the sweatshirt as he nodded.

"Can you get to the door or do you need me to help you?"

"I can do it." And she did. Barely. Back outside, the fresh sea breeze helped a little. Very little.

Watching Eric lock up the cabin, she gauged the distance to the dock and decided not to chance it without him. When he was done, he looked over at her with that odd combination of surprise and anger that she'd seen earlier.

"Let's get you on dry land."

She gestured to his sweatshirt, now cradled in the crook of his arm. "Let me wash that."

"Let's worry about getting you home first, Amy, and then we can talk about laundry." He moved her across the deck with ease, and had her standing on dry land. "Now into the truck."

"Really, Eric. I walked here and I can easily walk home." At the shake of Eric's head, Amy gave in and allowed him to help her inside. With the seat belt buckled and Eric trotting around the truck toward his door, she let out a sigh of relief. At least she'd made it this far without disgracing herself. Other than the ridiculous skinned knee and his stained sweatshirt.

The short drive to her home passed quickly, and soon her feet were standing somewhat steadily on the driveway. "Better?" Eric asked.

"Yes," she managed. For though the queasiness of her stomach and the stinging of her knee had lessened, now the heartache of Eric's indifference to her impending departure hit her.

"Amy?"

"I'm fine," she said as she pulled away from his grasp. "It was just a little seasickness and a skinned knee."

And a broken heart.

He stood firm. "I want to talk about the invitation. What was it you were inviting me here for? Was it because of my note? See, I—"

"It was just supposed to be dinner," she said quickly. "Nothing else. And there's no need to explain the note. We both knew my job was temporary, and I know you're a busy man. I appreciate that you could take the time to let me know." She tried not to wince at the potential for sarcasm in the words she'd so calmly spoken. "So, have you eaten?"

"Yes, at Gaido's." He shrugged. "I always meet Christy's parents there before I leave

the girls with them for a week at the beach."
His lip turned in the beginnings of a smile.
"Ironic that they leave the beach to go to the
beach, isn't it?" Eric paused. "Who am I kid-
ding? I don't want to talk about any of that.
Tell me about this job in San Antonio."

Amy's heart lurched. And yet she said nothing. Instead she searched his face for some
hint of how he felt about the topic.

"Something wrong?" he finally asked. "It's
a good job, right?"

A lift of his chin and Amy spied what appeared to be honest interest in the topic and
not a bit of regret. Not what she'd hoped.

"Yes," she said on a long exhale of breath.
"It's a very good job. A great job, actually."

"No multitasking, then?" he asked with a
chuckle.

Amy joined him in laughing though the attempt was a poor one. "One client at a time,"
she said as she toyed with the end of her
ponytail. "Or, rather, one wedding at a time."

At the mention of a wedding, Eric lifted
his gaze to meet hers then reached to touch
her hand. A reminder of their kisses taunted
Amy but, for the moment, she tucked it away.

Without a word, he led her around the path to the swing beneath the arbor. When she'd seated herself beside him, the familiar scent of roses and salt air comforted her racing heart. Slowly, she braved a glance in his direction.

Though his face was partially covered in shadow, Amy could see his direct stare bore no visible expression of concern. "All right," he said slowly as he leaned back against the ancient boards of the old swing, "now tell me more about the job."

She did, starting slowly in the hopes Eric might stop her and beg her to stay. Instead, he used her halting pauses to ask questions, or worse, to offer opinions on just how fabulous the opportunity sounded. "So," she said in closing, "most of my responsibilities will be in meeting clients—one at a time, as I said—and helping to plan the floral arrangements for their big day."

"When do you start?" he said, his voice hoarse.

"Soon as I want, actually," she said with what she hoped would be some measure of enthusiasm. "It's just a matter of finding a place to live. I thought I'd make a trip out there in a day or two and finalize the arrangements." She glanced around for effect. "It's not like I've got much to pack. Just my books and clothes. Everything else here is Nana's."

Eric ducked his head and, for a moment, Amy felt her hopes rising. *Tell me not to go,* she wanted to shout. *Tell me to stay and I will.*

But when he looked up and met her hopeful stare, Eric quickly looked past her. "I'm happy for you." And then he stood, shaking the swing with his hurried move. "You'll let me know if I can help with anything, won't you?"

"Help?" She shook her head. "What do you mean?"

He ran his hand through his dark hair then turned to stare out at the horizon. The salt-tinged breeze drifted past, lifting the hem of his pale blue shirt as the setting sun turned his tanned face a golden-bronze. Eric's eyes closed, and for a moment he appeared to be considering something with some measure of difficulty. Then, slowly, his eyes opened and he turned to face her.

Hope rose. Did Eric intend to declare his feelings? To beg her to stay?

"I mean, you know," he began, "I have a

truck so if you need any help moving, I'm your guy."

Amy's heart sank. She forced a smile in spite of the numbness that threatened to freeze her on the spot. "Yes, of course," she said with what she hoped would be enthusiasm. "I don't think that will be necessary."

And then, foolishly, she fell into an embrace that she knew would be their last. How had this happened? Where was the love she thought would keep her in Vine Beach?

When they parted, she quickly hid the glistening tears by turning her head. "Good night, Eric," she said as she hurried to the porch and slid inside. "And, goodbye," she whispered to the red taillights of the departing truck a few minutes later.

Like an idiot, Eric had embraced Amy when he'd known it would be the last time. Worse, he'd driven away without telling Amy it was killing him to let her go. Killing him to pretend he was happy for her promotion to the big time when he'd much rather she stayed here. And killing him that he had finally found love only to let it slip from his hands like the grains of sand on Vine Beach.

The light turned red, and Eric hit the brakes and stopped. The moon danced over Vine Beach, teasing the white tops of the breakers as they raced to shore. He hit the off button on the air conditioner and rolled his windows down to take in a healthy dose of salt air. Off in the distance he spied Sand Island, instantly taking him back to the moment he first kissed Amy.

One memory tumbled after the other and formed a long string of good reasons why he shouldn't let Amy go. Why he couldn't.

A horn honked, indicating the light had turned green. Eric swung the truck around and headed back in the opposite direction. The right one.

Maybe he wasn't such an idiot, after all.

# Chapter Twenty

Shrugging off the urge to either cry or call her mother or Nana, Amy sat her phone on the table chair, locked the door behind her and trudged upstairs to draw a bath. She had just tossed the last of her clothes on the floor and a handful of bath salt into the steaming water when the doorbell rang.

Throwing her clothes back on, Amy hurried downstairs. A glance through the peephole and she opened the door. "Eric? What are you doing here?"

He looked past her through the open door. "Can I come in?"

"Yes, sure, of course," she said as she ushered Eric in and then closed the door. "Wait,

I need to go turn off the bathwater." She ran back upstairs just in time to stop the tub from overflowing. A glance in the mirror told Amy she looked a fright. Between the seasickness and the salt air, her hair was a mess, and the tears she'd shed since Eric left hadn't helped, either.

Scrubbing her face and running a comb through her hair helped, but not by much. Finally she gave up and walked to the stairs. From where she stood, she could see Eric leaning against the mantel, his attention focused on a small silver photograph of Nana and Grandpa on their wedding day. With Grandpa looking dapper in his dress uniform and Nana trying her best to smile despite the fact her husband would be heading off to war the day after their honeymoon ended, it was Amy's favorite picture of her grandparents.

That Eric studied it so intently unsettled her almost as much as the fact he now stood in Nana's parlor. Her heart beating furiously, Amy rubbed her palms against her shorts and fixed a guarded expression on her face. "What are you doing here?"

Eric turned to face her. "You didn't answer the phone."

Amy turned to see the red light flashing on her phone. "I'm sorry about that. I just didn't…"

"Didn't want to talk to me?" he asked as he jammed his hands into his pockets.

"No," she said a bit too hastily. "I left it down here when I went up to take a bath."

He moved closer, his gaze locked with hers. "Are you happy here?"

"Happy?" came out sounding far away.

"Yes, happy," he said. "I'm really hoping that you're not leaving Vine Beach because you hate living here." He looked surprised that he'd said the words aloud then he shook his head. "I'm not making sense, am I?"

She opened her mouth to speak but found there were no words. *Lord, if You're going to do something, please hurry,* she managed to pray. "Not really," she finally managed.

Eric gathered her into his arms. "Amy," he said as he held her tight, "just the thought of you being so far away…"

He paused and seemed to be collecting his thoughts. Then he swung his gaze to collide with hers. Were those tears she saw threatening?

She slid from his grasp and moved toward the front window. From there she could see the lights of the wharf and the sailboats bobbing at anchor. Lifting her gaze to the heavens, she watched the moon slide behind a cloud, turning the water beneath it from silver to a deep midnight-blue.

Eric had come to stand beside her, but she dare not risk a peek. If his tears fell, so would hers. And then where would they be? Two fools who couldn't say they loved each other but couldn't stand the thought of being apart.

Or maybe just one fool. Her.

"Eric," she said softly, "I don't want to leave things unsaid."

From the corner of her eye she could see him nodding as he stared out into the darkness. "We've left too many things unsaid, haven't we?"

Abruptly his fingers encircled her wrist and drew her to him. Instead of embracing her, Eric twirled her around as if they were doing a waltz to some imaginary tune. They stopped in front of the mantel, and Eric held her tight to his chest.

"I love you, Amy Spencer," he said against her ear. "I love you," he repeated when he moved back just enough to meet her stare.

Amy's heart melted, and the tears she'd held back began to flow.

"Did I say something wrong?" he asked as he used his thumb to whisk away a tear. "Please don't cry."

"I love you, too," she said as she rested her head on his chest.

"You do?" His voice rumbled against her ear.

"Of course I do, Eric."

His laughter bubbled up and echoed in the parlor. "Please don't leave. Stay with me." He held her out at arm's length. "Forever."

Another tear fell. Amy ignored it. "Forever?"

"Forever." Eric released her to reach for the photograph of Nana and Grandpa. "I want us to grow old together like they did. And someday when I look back I want to say that I didn't make the dumbest mistake of my life and let you go plan other people's weddings."

Her heart fluttered as her hands began to shake. "What are you saying?"

He returned the picture to the mantel then dropped to one knee before her. "Plan *our* wedding," he said. "Go all-out. Do whatever you want, but marry me, Amy. Please?"

Amy wasted no time in arranging the perfect wedding for the second week of August. They would say their vows in Nana's rose garden with Riley Burkett officiating.

Under Nana's supervision, and with Susan Wilson's help, the ladies at the assisted-living facility had flown into action to create the menu for the occasion. At Eric's request, the wedding guests would be served Nana's delicious coconut cake, and, because the girls wanted it, porch salad would also be prepared. She'd found the perfect wedding dress in a trunk in Nana's attic, and when she tried it on, Amy found the dress from the picture in the silver frame on the mantel fit her as if it had been made for her.

The morning of the wedding dawned bright and cloudless. Amy went out at first light to check the garden and found the blooms were drooping from the heat. She turned on the sprinkler one last time before the Eric's friends from the Starting Over group came to set up chairs in the garden.

The task accomplished, Amy brought the sprinkler into the backyard to gently water the parched grass while she went inside to prepare for the day. Soon Ima arrived to do her hair, followed by Susan, who brought Nana and the ladies who would serve the food. Behind them was Riley and the Starting Over guys, who were quickly called into service to unload the mountain of food the ladies had prepared.

All of this Amy observed from the bedroom upstairs where she'd been sent to don her wedding dress. When the knock came at the door, she gathered up her flowers and the tiny copy of the New Testament her parents had given her last night.

"Amy?" a chorus of little voices called.

She smiled and opened the door to her three pint-size bridesmaids. "Girls, you look beautiful!"

Their wide eyes and broad smiles sent Amy's heart soaring. The girls wore soft pink, girlish versions of Amy's white satin wedding gown, and the two older girls carried pastel flowers decorated with pink ribbons. Little Brooke carried a pink basket filled with white rose petals and bedecked with the same pick ribbons her sisters carried.

"Skipper's got his brand-new collar on," Brooke said.

"That's wonderful, sweetheart," Amy responded.

Amy caught her father looking up at her from the bottom of the stairs. He seemed to have difficulty speaking before he finally managed to say, "It's time, Amy. Are you ready?"

She met him at the bottom of the stairs. "I am."

They walked together to the front door where Mama and Susan awaited. "Beautiful," Mama said.

"Oh, honey." She turned to see Nana coming through the kitchen door, her purse dangling from the crook of her arm. Her grandmother stopped to place her hands on Amy's cheeks. "Darling, the sight of you brings me back to the day I married your grandpa."

Amy smiled as she tucked the handkerchief around the base of the flowers.

The front door opened a crack and Riley Burkett peered in. "Ready?" he asked.

"Yes," Amy said. "Absolutely."

"Now, let's go have a wedding."

The ladies went first, followed by the two oldest Wilson girls. Just before Brooke was to make her way up the aisle, Eric's best friend, Jeremy Holt, came around the corner with Skipper. The dog's leash had been decorated with pink ribbons, likely against Eric's protests, and a pink pillow with two gold rings had been affixed to his collar.

The handsome aviator looked less than pleased. "I know it's not traditional, but Eric thought it might be a good idea if I walk the dog down the aisle instead of Brooke."

Amy covered her smile with her hand. "What do you think, Brooke?"

Brooke reached for her, pulling Amy down to her eye level. "Long as you get to be my new mommy."

"Absolutely, sweetheart." Tears threatened as she hugged the little girl then sent her on her way. By the time she took her father's arm and made her way toward the garden, she'd almost tamed them. Then she spied Eric standing beside Riley and they began to fall again.

Somehow she traversed the aisle to stand between Dad and Eric. Just as Riley finished the opening prayer, Skipper managed to escape. Thankfully, he slipped beneath the hedge toward the backyard where he could likely play happily until the ceremony ended.

Riley continued with a grin, and soon he was proclaiming them husband and wife. "You may kiss your bride, Eric."

"Gladly," he said as he gathered Amy into an embrace and offered up a scorching kiss. A cheer went up, along with clapping when Eric maneuvered her into a dip and gave her another kiss.

Then the crowd went wild. And then, from the clear blue sky, rain began to fall.

Eric straightened and set Amy steady on her feet just as the source of the precipitation ran past. Following the lovely silk runner that Brooke had decorated with her rosebuds, Skipper was making muddy footprints as the sprinkler in his mouth doused the wedding guests.

Only when the hose reached its length did he release his prize. The sprinkler landed in the center of the aisle, the water reaching both the bride's and groom's guests with equal measure.

Eric made to follow the dog, but Amy caught his wrist and began to laugh. A moment later, his irritated expression melted to a smile as he nodded to Riley.

"Ladies and gentlemen," Riley said to the guests, who now huddled at the edges of the garden, safe from the sprinkler but damp from their efforts, "I'm pleased to introduce Dr. and Mrs. Eric Wilson."

The guests began to clap as Eric offered Amy his arm and together they walked down the aisle. Just shy of the reach of the sprinkler Eric paused. "I'd thought this might come later in the evening," he said to Amy, "but may I have this dance, Mrs. Wilson?"

And together, they stepped into the circle of water while the cameras flashed. The next day, a somewhat familiar headline appeared in the next edition of the *Vine Creek Gazette* along with a photograph of the newlyweds dancing beneath the sparkling downpour. This time, the words were slightly different: Daddy's Little Matchmakers Make Their Match.

* * * * *

Dear Reader,

When I started planning the tale of Amy and Eric, I had no idea I would be writing the book during one of the coldest winters on record. Imagine writing about warm sunshine and sandy beaches in Texas when the snowy Oklahoma landscape is all you can see out the window. And yet, I grew to love the fictional town of Vine Beach and the people who populate the little city on the Texas shore, even as I shivered and tried to keep warm.

You see, I grew up not too far from a beach very much like Vine Beach. As I grew older, summers were spent collecting shells and playing in the surf, a love I never quite outgrew. There's just something wonderful about sitting on the sand with the waves rolling in and looking out over the wide expanse of God's watery creation that soothes a beach-lover's soul and makes the world feel very small.

I hope that you'll feel the same way as you read about Amy's search for something permanent and Eric's quest to understand how different can be equally good. And as you read about the love of family, about God's timing and how He is never late nor is He early, I hope that you will hold on to His promises and know He cares about your every need.

Prayers are as plentiful as the grains of sand on the ocean, and yet God hears every one. My prayer as you read this book is that you, too, will know what it is to feel the love of the Lord and to know His are the only arms worth falling into.

I look forward to hearing from my readers, and hope that you will drop me a line at Love Inspired Books, 233 Broadway, Suite 1001, New York, NY 10279, or through my website at www.kathleenybarbo.com.

Wishing you all the best!
*Kathleen Y'Barbo*

# QUESTIONS FOR DISCUSSION

1. Amy feels her life is on hold until the Lord gives her something to do that isn't temporary. Have you ever felt as if you were playing a waiting game with God? What do you do while you're waiting?

2. Eric struggles with knowing how to live again after his wife's death. His is a tragedy that he can't seem to get past even though those who love him most are trying to help. Have you faced a struggle seemingly so insurmountable you felt there was no solution? What did you do? How did you get past it?

3. Eric feels that Amy can't possibly be the woman God wants him to marry because she is so different from his late wife. He cannot understand God's logic in pairing him with someone who is not what he planned. Has the Lord ever surprised you by doing something completely unpredictable? What was it and how did you react?

4. When Amy is faced with the possibility of finally seeing Sand Island, she allows fear to almost keep her from going. What is it you would like to do but are afraid of trying? Can you do as Amy did and figure out a way to conquer your fear? If so, how?

5. Amy's prayer, and occasionally Eric's, was to plead for God to hurry. Have you ever prayed that prayer? If so, how did it turn out? Were you able to see later that the Lord's timing was much better than yours?

6. Eric's daughters loved him enough to take drastic measures to see that he was happy again. Have you been faced with a friend who needed your help? How did you go about helping them, and what were the results?

7. Amy battles seasickness, so when she knows she is going to sail, she plans ahead. Are there things in your life you know will be a

problem, things you have to plan ahead to be prepared for? What are they and how do you prepare for them?

8. Eric is reluctant to join the Starting Over group at his church, but later finds good Christian friends there. Have you ever paused before doing something that turned out well? Or, conversely, is there something you wish you'd done sooner?

9. Eric's mother and daughters love him very much and want the best for him. Because of this, they take a big risk. Have you ever taken a risk for a friend? What was the result?

10. The Bible says that God's plans are not our own. This was certainly true for both Amy and Eric. How has this been true in your life?

11. Eric leaves the big city and gives up his veterinary practice to move back home to Vine Beach in order to give his daughters what he prays will be a better life. What

changes can you make today that will improve your life or the lives of those you love?

12. Amy has happy memories of traditions such as porch salad, which have been handed down from her grandmother. Do you have favorite traditions that you are passing on? If not, what can you do today to create family traditions that are repeated in future generations?

13. Amy went from being a single woman to wife and mother of three. How do you handle big life changes that you come across?

14. Which scene was your favorite and why?

15. What did you think of Susan trying to play matchmaker?